I0571299

Triple Diamond

THE LOVIN' IS EASY

GEMMA SNOW

The Lovin' is Easy
ISBN # 978-1-913186-12-8
©Copyright Gemma Snow 2017
Cover Art by Posh Gosh ©Copyright August 2017
Interior text design by Claire Siemaszkiewicz
Totally Bound Publishing

THE LOVIN'
IS EASY

Dedication

To Mary, for being as excited about a Montana
ranch series as I am.
Always to my family, always to Robbie. I couldn't
do any of this without you guys.

Chapter One

"A *what?*"

Against the din of the ancient window air conditioner chugging into the room, Madison's voice had a tinny, almost petulant sound. But of all the things she had expected from the impromptu meeting with some family estate lawyer she'd never heard of, *this* wasn't it.

"A *ranch*, Ms. Hollis," Mr. Sidney replied, the tone of his voice indicating that he'd picked up on her confusion and ensuing frustration with the afternoon's events and that, frankly, he didn't care. "The Triple Diamond Ranch in Wolf Creek, Montana, to be exact."

Madison rubbed her hands over her face and tried to make sense of everything. Mr. Sidney had contacted her a week prior about a will left to her by some uncle on her mother's side, an uncle she'd never heard of, from a mother who'd been gone some eighteen years now. She took a deep breath, trying a different tack.

"Are you certain this is my uncle" — she glanced at the stack of legal documents two inches thick on the desk before her — "Mason?"

Mr. Sidney peered down at her over the wire rim of his thin glasses — a remarkable feat, given that she had at least two inches on the man, who sat short and boney in the chair across the desk.

"Mr. Mason Westerly King first arranged this inheritance with Sidney and Sidney nearly two decades ago," he replied. "We've had ample time to determine and confirm your identity, Ms. Hollis."

Madison resisted the urge to roll her eyes, but only just. Mr. Sidney's attitude came on the tail of what had already been the week from hell. She sighed, her heavy breath spilling out of her mouth like a deflating hot air balloon. *It's only Wednesday.*

"Mr. Sidney, I'm afraid I still don't quite understand. What am I supposed to do with a ranch" — she gestured with her hand — "I don't know, eight, ten hours away from here?"

He gave a slow blink. "My advice, Ms. Hollis, is to go inspect the ranch yourself. You have all the information on the mineral rights and past financial records. Once you get the lay of the land, you can determine whether you wish to sell or keep the property. But otherwise, after I get your signature on these forms, I'm afraid there's not much else I can help you with."

Madison did scowl that time, but with her head bent over the stack of papers while signing the requisite lines, he couldn't see it. She was perfectly pleased to be done with Mr. Sidney for good, but he was wrong about one major thing. She wasn't going to decide whether or not to keep the ranch — she had decided the very first time he had mentioned the word *inheritance.* No, the second she got out to Montana, she would sell the damn thing and be done with it. Maybe then everything would go back to normal. *Ha. Yeah, right.*

Chapter Two

Ryder Dean took the steps to the kitchen two at a time, tugging his worn gray Ford shirt over his head as he did. When he reached the landing, he beelined for the coffee pot and inhaled the rich, inviting flavor that hit his senses when he poured a generous cup. Only after he had downed half the mug did he lean back against the counter to look over at the island, where Christian switched between leafing through an old Harley-Davidson catalog and peering up at him with a sardonic expression.

"When did Caleigh take off?" Ryder asked. He plucked a piece of bacon off the pan on the stovetop and popped into his mouth.

Christian shrugged and hid his face behind his dark hair, glancing back down at the magazine.

"I've been up since four and she was gone. Probably right after you passed out like a drunken donkey."

Ryder rolled his eyes. "It's not my fault she left. You know how she is—never stayed the night, never will." He was reaching for another piece of bacon when both of their phones buzzed at the same time, signaling an incoming text. Ryder dug his cell out of the back pocket of his worn jeans and slid the screen awake. Sure enough, it was from Caleigh, in a group message to him and Christian.

Just wanted to say thanks for last night. I did a lot of thinking and I've decided to go for it — booked my plane for New York, leaving Sunday. If you ever make it that far east, look me up. X – C

Ryder sloshed more coffee into his mug and re-read the text message, pursing his lips in amusement when the words sunk in.

"Well, I'll be damned," he said. "Guess we were *too* good at being shoulders to cry on."

He typed out a quick response.

Don't forget us when you're famous. Best of luck.

Christian let out a low chuckle. "She's going to be an actress one way or another, Ry, just never in Montana." He took a long swig from his own coffee cup. "I will miss her, though."

It was funny, that. Christian didn't look like the kind of guy to admit to feeling something unless he was under the knife. With long dark hair that nearly reached his shoulders, spirals and stories of ink covering both arms, shoulders and much of his back, he was rebel country and riding the highway to hell. Ryder would know — he'd seen most of the journey from the front seat. But between the two of them, Ryder had always been the first to lock up anything sticky, emotional or rough, not Christian, the resident bad boy. But what the hell, they'd been surprising people near twenty years at this point. There was no reason to stop now.

"That's 'cause she liked you more than me," he shot back, turning to the coffee pot and finding it empty. He glanced at the clock. It was already quarter after five, not enough time for another pot, so he soaped up the coffee mug in the sink instead.

Christian laughed out loud at that. "Only 'cause I'm better at eating pussy than you."

Ryder lobbed the wet sponge at him. It landed with a soapy *plop* a good two feet away from where Christian sat. *Damn it.*

"I'll let you think that," he said. "But next time we bring a girl home, be sure to ask her."

Christian chucked the sponge right back at his head and Ryder dodged. This time, it smacked into the picture window, leaving a soapy trail as it slid to the countertop.

"I know you're not being a prick 'cause Caleigh took off after we spent the whole night telling her to *follow her dreams*, so what's up your ass today, Ry?"

Ryder pursed his lips. They'd caught Caleigh Sullivan at McLean's Bar the night before, three shots of top shelf whiskey deep. Caleigh had gone to the same middle and high schools as Ryder and Christian and they'd known her almost as long as they'd known each other. That was just the way of Wolf Creek.

When they'd finally got her talking, Caleigh hadn't stopped — her fears about becoming another townie, about never pursuing her dreams, about what might happen if she failed. They had returned to the house Ryder and Christian shared on the Triple Diamond Ranch and, apparently, convinced Caleigh that it was the right idea to go to New York. There hadn't been much talking after that, just stripping down and showing her all the best parts of Wolf Creek. But it wasn't the impromptu threesome with Caleigh that had Ryder's nerves running high. He and Christian had traversed that territory before and they would again.

"New owner's coming around today," he said after a moment, walking over to the window that looked out across three thousand green and blue sprawling acres of horse ranch and farm. "Who knows, maybe we'll be on a plane to New York this Sunday, too." Not that either of them would fit in in the big city – any big city.

Trepidation crossed Christian's expression and Ryder nodded. Ever since they had found Mason in the barn a month before, the knowledge that their future was uncertain had remained a heavy weight on Ryder's shoulders. Of course, it was nowhere near the guilt he felt at not having been there to save the life of the man who had become a surrogate uncle to him these past fifteen years, but it was there all the same. Would the Triple Diamond go to the state, or some relative they'd never met?

None of that changed the fact that he and Christian were less than four weeks short of buying part ownership in the ranch – at a heavily reduced price – a promise Mason had offered them both when they turned eighteen, if they'd agreed to get college degrees and come work for him for five years. Twelve years later and they were just a few grand lean of the agreed price – and a few weeks too late. Now, the fate of Triple Diamond, Mason Westerly King's legacy and their jobs hung in a very delicate balance.

Christian came over to the window and slipped his mug into the sink. Then he, too, stared out over the vastness of Triple Diamond, many of the same thoughts in Ryder's mind likely crossing his own.

"Any idea when he's coming?" Christian asked. The weight of the reminder settled a physical tension on the room. *Will this even still be our kitchen tomorrow?*

"No clue," Ryder replied. "Estate lawyer just said the new owner would be arriving today." He took one last long, lingering glance out at the familiar scene, then clapped Christian on the back. "Come on, we've got work to do." And wasn't that just the way of it — the harder things got, the harder they worked. That was how they'd always survived and it sure as shit wasn't about to change now.

* * * *

It was fucking hot. Ryder had been in the barn for half the afternoon with three pregnant mares that were all ready to pop. Two of the pregnancies were coming along well, but the third mare, a beautiful Tennessee Walker named Sasha, had acted agitated and uncomfortable. Given that it was the first really hot week of the year, he'd examined her out of an overabundance of caution, but a closer look had shown signs of an infected placenta, which had caused their horses to lose foals in the past. He had put her on a strict regimen of antibiotics and she had seemed to calm a little, which was a good sign.

But, since life never stopped, he'd made his rounds through the barn for minor ailments and injuries, then joined Christian who was out in a nearby field looking over their irrigation ditches. It was late June and it was hot, but in Montana summer came late and ran high then left town without so much as a by-your-leave. Though they'd planted almost everything for the season, Christian hadn't finalized the last section, and he was standing peering out over the land when Ryder approached.

"Any last-minute changes?" Ryder kicked up dirt with every step. *Damn.* They could use at least one good rain before planting, but as the old saying went, *if you don't like the weather, wait a minute.*

"I'm considering switching Zone Four and Zone Two." Christian looked down at the large blueprint he held. "We sold better on nightshades last year, right?"

Ryder shrugged. If anyone would know the answer to that question, it was Christian. The guy's head for numbers boggled Ryder's mind, so he didn't say anything, just leaned back against the wooden fence and wiped the sweat off his brow. *Damn, it's hot in the barn.* The industrial ceiling fan had broken at the end of fall and there hadn't been reason to fix it. Now, it was priority number one. He rubbed the rest of his face with his shirt then recoiled.

"Damn, I smell like horse," he said. Groaning when the muscles in his back popped and stretched, he pulled the soiled shirt off his head. What he needed was a shower to get some of the stench of pregnant, ticked-off horse out of his hair and skin, but there were several fences on this line alone that needed mending and he had inventory to run in the barn and tool shed. It was officially past spring-cleaning.

But before he got the chance to tell Christian where he was headed, he caught sight of something in the distance. The Triple Diamond Ranch was only accessible by private road, a road visible from damn near anywhere on the three thousand acres. The driver was making good time, given the wave of dust kicking up around the white speck of car. At that speed, it wasn't any of their hands — those guys knew way better than to drive that fast on the dirt road. Which could only mean…

"Damn," Ryder muttered. He chucked the dirty shirt over one shoulder. "There's no way I have time to shower before that speed freak gets down here."

Christian chuckled. Even with the Jack Daniels tank, oversized belt buckle and Stetson, Christian was all biker—from the tats winding up and down his arms to the aviator sunglasses low on his nose. *Speed freak* was one of Ryder's favorite nicknames for him.

"Fuck it, man." Christian folded the blueprint and pocketed it. "When you inherit a farm, workers smelling like horse shit are part of the bargain."

Ryder glanced over at the approaching car, then slapped Christian on the back.

"You're right," he said, "Let's go see what's in store for us."

They made their way out of the fields and past the barn and walked the short distance to Holmwood Manor. It had been Mason's house—a mansion, really—though Ryder had always thought it a little depressing that Mason had lived alone in such a large place. It was like a reminder of just how alone he'd been and that he'd never married or had any kids, at least as far as Ryder knew. Still, Holmwood was gorgeous. Tucked away under several large maple trees, it was the kind of place a guy went to escape the troubles of the world. Hell, *all* Triple Diamond was.

They reached the driveway before the car, though judging by the encroaching dust storm, it wasn't by much. Ryder leaned back against the wooden fence that lined the drive and breathed in the sweet, rich scent of summer in the mountains—fresh water and pine and turned-up dirt from the crops. He couldn't leave the ranch. Triple Diamond was the only place he'd ever really belonged.

The car took one final corner and pulled up the small incline in a cloud of dust. The dirt slowly settled and Ryder blinked to clear his vision. A BMW. *Fuck*. Anyone who had ever even *been* to a ranch would know how out of place a car like that was. A truck like his old Ford was the best bet, and the ranch hands drove Jeeps or SUVS. But a two-seater Beemer convertible? They were in deep shit.

Then the door to the sports car opened and one foot slid out, landing in the dust. The foot wore a red high heel, at least three inches tall and skinny as a pencil. Ryder glanced over at Christian, who wore an expression of disbelief.

So close. They had been so close to buying ownership in Triple Diamond. But something in Ryder's gut said that whoever was attached to that red high-heeled foot was about to stir up trouble in his life the likes of which he'd never before seen.

Chapter Three

Madison didn't know what to expect from her visit to the Triple Diamond Ranch. Life in Silicon Valley, barely an hour away from Chinatown, where she'd grown up, hadn't prepared her for the vast openness, the rising mountains or sprawling sky of the Montana landscape. It was about forty minutes from the airport, which had given Madison ample time to see the unfamiliar state and to double down on her plans of selling the strange inheritance as fast as possible. She was *not* the kind of person to own a place like this.

Case in point—the white Beemer she'd picked up from the car rental had smeared brown and red within ten seconds of driving and the guy in the gas station had laughed his ass off when questioned about the nearest car wash. Still, she did have to admit that the wide, open stretches of highway with no other cars in sight were a nice break from the grueling traffic and perpetual congestion of downtown San Francisco. While taking the roads to Triple Diamond Ranch too quickly, she'd mulled over just how much easier her role of event planning manager for Daniels and Hark for the Valley's tech titans would be if she could get across town in less time than it took to get what felt like halfway across the state.

But now she was here, if the large, cast-iron sign of three diamonds surrounded by mountains on both sides and a large *TD* in curling script she had passed was any indication. Okay, so the view from the drive up to what Mr. Sidney had referred to as Holmwood Manor was beautiful. She hadn't seen that much sky in a long time, not since the occasional camping trip in college. But the blasts of dirt encircling her and wide stretches of nothingness were unsettling. She just wasn't accustomed to this much quiet or fresh air or peaceful empty space.

With a heavy sigh, Madison killed the ignition. The sooner she got this whole thing over with, the sooner everything in her life would return to normal. Well, not *everything*. But the call from Mr. Sidney and the frantic flight to Montana, of all places, not to mention, the insane work hours she kept, longer this week to prepare for her trip, had busied her enough to temporarily forget Joshua and the scene she had walked in on less than a week ago.

Whatever. One problem at a time.

She tossed her phone into her oversized purse, scooped the bag across her shoulder and stepped out of the car, slamming the door behind her.

And stopped dead in her tracks.

The poster boy for pretty country leaned against the wooden fence a few feet from her car, his bare chest on display for all to see—and *whoa, baby,* there was a hell of a lot to see—with a T-shirt slung over one shoulder and his worn jeans riding low on his hips. His hair was short and blonde and his blue eyes sparkled with amusement, undoubtedly at her expense for one reason or another.

But there wasn't just one staggeringly hot stud suddenly making it all kinds of hard for Madison to breathe. Next to cowboy cliché sat his total opposite. This man definitely wasn't *pretty*. His black hair curled against his shoulders, where swirls of rich ink adorned skin tanned dark from the sun. He wore a pair of reflective aviator sunglasses, but rather than minimizing Madison's sensation of being scrutinized, they heightened it.

Compared to their cotton tanks and faded jeans, her pencil skirt and form-fitting button-down felt wildly out of place. The red high heels she'd thought so cute when dressing that morning were for the San Fran event-planning manager and not the crumbling dirt driveway of a Montana ranch.

Stupid, Madison, stupid. Of course, she'd been thinking that a lot lately.

But she refused to go anywhere near *that* topic of conversation, so she pushed aside her insecurities, squared her shoulders and strode over to the two men. The man with the long hair was definitely the more intimidating of the two, his expression stormy and intense even from behind the mirrored glasses. So, she smiled at him and stuck out her hand to pretty boy first.

"Madison Hollis," she said. He molded his hand into her grip more gently than she'd anticipated, sliding the professional greeting into something intimate. Quickly, she pulled her hand away and extended it to tall, dark and dangerous. That wasn't any better. His rough, calloused hands stroked her mind with totally insane fantasies of how they might feel caressing the rest of her skin. "I'm looking for Ryder Dean and Christian Harlow."

She didn't miss the way pretty boy looked her up and down, nor her body's vibrating response of at his perusal, despite her best efforts to ignore it.

"You found 'em," he said. "I'm Ryder, this is Christian." The other man nodded and Ryder continued, "What can we do ya for?" His smooth roll of an accent dragged her attention to the soft bob of his Adam's apple in the column of his throat that led to a very bare, very muscled chest. It was sun-soaked and…

Get it together, Madison.

"I'm the new owner," she said. It came out more like a question. Funny that, it was her very first time saying the statement out loud. "I believe we have some things to discuss."

Understatement of the fucking millennium. She'd seen pictures of the ranch before coming out, of course, but Triple Diamond went *way* beyond anything she could have ever imagined. It was massive, staggeringly beautiful and just overwhelming. There was suddenly more acreage in her name than ten city blocks in San Francisco. It was a lot to take in.

Christian tilted his chin, looking over the edge of his aviator glasses and giving her a glimpse into the mysterious, penetrating eyes below the reflective frames. *Oh, yeah, definitely intimidating. Definitely tempting.*

"Are you certain you're in the right place, Ms. Hollis?" he asked, and while his voice wasn't outright rude, it certainly wasn't welcoming either.

Ryder slapped Christian on the back and stepped away from the fence.

"What he means is, I don't believe we've ever seen a ranch owner wearing high heels before," he said with a grin. "Most folks around here are the shit-kicker-boots type, if you'll pardon my language, ma'am."

Oh, he's really laying it on thick, isn't he? And you're eating it up.

Ryder indicated the manor house with a tilt of his head and Christian hopped—if a man like him ever *hopped*—down from the fence, his gaze never leaving Madison. She felt it like the heat from the sun—a warm, dangerous caress, one she shouldn't want more of, but that left her feeling flushed and not a little sexy.

"I'm from San Francisco," she said, hoisting her purse up higher on her shoulder, suddenly feeling the absurd need to explain herself. "We don't exactly have an excess of dirt roads." Without waiting for a reply, she unlocked the trunk of the car to reveal her large Vera Wang traveling duffel. A little unsteady on the now-totally-insane-idea thin heels in the packed dirt, she crossed over to the car to get it and slung the large bag over her free shoulder.

Madison didn't miss the look both men shot her way. Fine, so she was an outsider. *So what?* But her self-consciousness disappeared when they grew closer to the house. It was a gorgeous three-story mansion in shades of red and white and she ached to be inside its cool walls. She was so focused on the soft, ageless beauty of the home that she dug her heel into the dirt at a bad angle and stumbled against the dry ground, almost losing her footing.

Christian brought his arm around her waist in an instant, steadying her until she could pull her damn shoe free.

"Whoa, there." He looked, if possible, more irritated than he had when she first arrived and Madison resisted the urge to shake him off. Or maybe it was because his touch, simple though it was—nothing more intimate than one stranger helping another—made her ache, even with the barrier of shirt between them, and she felt his power in an overwhelming and confusing way. A spark of desire kindled deep in her belly, far deeper than her frustration at his less-than-warm welcome, and her breath caught in her throat.

As if burned, Christian stepped away from her, but held one hand out.

"Let me carry your bag."

He was definitely annoyed with her. A grimace caught at the edges of his lips, twisting and dangerous. When Madison handed him her duffel — heavy with a dozen stacks of files and legal documents — she wondered what he would look like if he smiled. Dazzling. Dangerous.

Oh, God, oh, God. Soooo not the time, Madison.

The rest of the short walk continued quietly, but Madison's internal monologue ran in a continuous stream of confusion and kindling desire. Confusion, because she couldn't quite figure out which of the two drop-dead-sexy cowboys at her side set off alarms bells, and double confusion because from where she stood, it was kind of, sort of *both*?

A moment later, Ryder unlocked the back door to Holmwood and indicated for her to lead them inside. The door let into a beautiful country kitchen, done up in blues and whites, with soft gingham curtains and rustic wooden details. Madison hadn't spent much time in the countryside, but this kitchen was everything she'd ever pictured it to be. All it needed now was a pie cooling on the windowsill.

"You can't stay here, since we turned off the electricity and water," Ryder said, as Christian placed her bag down on a seat near the table none too gently. "But we'll give you the tour and you can crash in the guest bedroom at our place. Do you want to see some of the land before we talk business?"

"That's not a bad idea, actually," Madison said, her breathing suddenly shallow at the thought of spending the night in the same house as the two cowboys. The kitchen wasn't small by any stretch, but with the enormous men taking up all the cool air to breathe and making her mind wander to the improper uses for a kitchen table, getting back out into the open air would probably be the best way for her to focus on what needed to be done. *Which is everything.*

"Do you have another pair of shoes?" Christian asked, his voice skeptical, though she didn't miss his perusing gaze sliding down the expanse of her leg to where it met the tall, stupidly thin red heels.

Madison nodded. "I've got my running shoes," she said, unzipping the duffel Christian had placed on the chair to root through it.

"You're killing me here, Ms. Hollis," Ryder put in, his tone genuinely humorous and kind, even as he mocked her. He opened a door she hadn't seen, just off to the right of the kitchen entrance, and poked around for a minute before finding a pair of boots.

"Think these will fit you?" he asked. "Just until we can buy you a new pair? You can't go walking around a ranch in June in a pair of sneakers. They'll be ruined in three minutes."

Madison rolled her eyes but accepted his logic and the boots. To her surprise, they were the perfect size, and when she slid them onto her feet, they were comfortable and secure. They decidedly did not match the tight pencil skirt or the form-fitting blouse she wore, both items from the very large *work clothes* section of her closet and so strong a part of her that Madison wasn't even sure she remembered how to dress another way. Not anymore.

But she pushed that surprisingly depressing thought aside and headed toward the door.

"Let's go," she said with a smile, "before I fall asleep on my feet." She was out of the door and back in the summer sun before either of the men and felt a small sense of satisfaction at being just half a step ahead of them. Something about both of them, Christian with his dark, simmering gaze, Ryder with the sexy masquerade covering the depths below, made her curious and interested — far more than she had any right to be. Especially since Ryder seemed nothing more than friendly and Christian was being a downright ass. And yet...they intrigued her, for some reason or another.

Yeah, it has nothing at all to do with how hot both of them are, does it?

Nothing at all. I'm just tired and they just happen to be here. And very hot.

Now that *she* was here, nearly eight hours after she had started her day, the fatigue was setting in, but she didn't have time to feel tired, at least not yet. *Best to just get started. On business. Just business. The business kind of business.*

They followed, far more slowly, clearly not as excited to begin a tour of the several-thousand-mile ranch. Or maybe the lack of excitement had more to do with the company — not something Madison felt like reading into, not with all the lack of *good company* vibes she'd gotten from Joshua this week. Still, she could deal with pissy men. It was the ones who put on façades and told people everything was just fine that made it difficult for her.

"It's a good look," Ryder said, the grin on his face belying the false compliment, and self-consciousness washed over her.

He's just being friendly. I do look ridiculous, wearing cowboy boots and a pencil skirt. He is not Joshua.

And yet, after two years and one shitty breakup, it was a challenge not to let the insidious voice of her ex-*fiancé* slip into her mind and root around.

"This was your idea," Madison said, trying to keep her voice neutral and not telling of the depths of her hurt. *Nope, back to business, please and thank you.* "Now, if you don't mind my asking, how is it that I'm communicating with you guys? What are your roles on the Triple Diamond Ranch?"

Maybe it was rude, but she had a lot questions and it was unlikely she'd be able to get out to Montana again soon, what with work being what it always was. Her current time off had been hard-won and she had been optimistic in not booking a return flight, hoping she wouldn't need the whole week to get a sale into motion. *Ha, fuck work if they can't take a joke.* Forget the paperwork—just one look at the Triple Diamond Ranch could tell any novice that the money she'd make from the sale would ensure she would never have to work again.

Then what will you do with yourself, Ms. Workaholic?

Spending a summer doing those two cowboys sounds pretty nice…

"We run the joint," Christian said, stating a simple fact, the only thing he'd said to her without attitude since she'd arrived. He slid the aviator glasses up into his hair and just as she'd thought, his eyes ran deep and intense. In fact, the expression in his dark brown gaze could have very nearly been read as an invitation. *No, that would be absurd.* Everything about this guy screamed irritation and annoyance, not promises and challenges.

Ryder came over to stand beside Madison, and though she could barely see him out of the corner of her eye, his presence made her tingle just as much as Christian's. Intense, if a little more playful, Ryder had the country-boy charm down to a science. A very alluring science.

"Christian and I started working here the summer we turned fourteen," Ryder explained. He guided her down the path and away from Holmwood Manor, Christian beside them, practically vibrating in his quiet irritation. "When we graduated high school, Mason gave us the option to go to college on his dime — if we promised to work the ranch for five years. I got my livestock vet degree and Christian focused on agricultural engineering, then we came back to the ranch full time. Mason made that offer twelve years ago and we never left, even after the five-year mark. So he started handing off more and more of the ranch duties to us." Ryder grinned. "Old man always said we had potential."

That was a lot to take in, so Madison just nodded, now even less sure of what to make of the two very intelligent, very sexy cowboys walking her into the barn of some unknown uncle's enormous ranch.

"If you don't mind my asking," she said, trying to turn back to business, the real kind of business, *thank you very much*, "Why didn't he just leave the farm to you two?"

Beside her, Ryder and Christian exchanged loaded looks, and Madison wondered if they were so adept at wordless communication in all aspects of their lives. Images of slicked-down muscles and long, thick... *Madison!*

"His death was unexpected," Ryder said, when they neared the barn door. "And Mason wanted Triple

Diamond to stay in the family. He was always very clear about that."

Madison shook her head, for several reasons, but it didn't clarify anything.

"I never even knew I had an uncle Mason," she said after a moment, pausing to step over the wooden doorframe and into the barn. "How I can be family?" Well, that wasn't exactly the right question to ask. After the car crash when she'd been ten, her dad's brother and sister-in-law had legally adopted her and she'd grown up as a sister to her cousin Lily. While she knew all about her dad's family, her mother had been the only tie to that side's history. Her grandparents were gone and her mom had never had any brothers or sisters, or so Madison had believed. She was suddenly very aware of the important connection Triple Diamond had to her family.

"Do you ride?" Ryder asked, indicating the horse that Madison only just realized hovered over her. Instinctively, she took a step away from it. It wasn't that she was afraid of horses, per se. It was just that she didn't feel inclined to go anywhere near one, especially not in this stupider-by-the-minute tight skirt she was wearing.

Never taking her eyes off the horse, she replied, "I haven't had much opportunity...to learn how to ride. Not too many horse barns in the Bay Area."

"Stables," Christian corrected. "You can ride with me. We're better off than walking and the battery in the golf cart is dead."

Madison smiled, but she couldn't deny that it came out more like a grimace. Even the surprisingly kind offer wasn't enough to make her want to hop on a horse.

"Of course it is," she mumbled mostly to herself. Jesus Christ, a week ago she'd woken up with a great job and a fiancé. Now she was standing in God only knew what, about to climb onto the back of a horse.

Christian led two horses, smaller than the one in front of her, out of a different stall and started loading leather saddles and reins onto them. She thought. She'd seen enough cowboy movies to hear the terms without actually knowing what they meant. He looked so at ease, so much calmer with the animals than he had been since she'd arrived. *Funny that, big strong man, put off by me. Ha.* He finished the task in quick, practiced motions then he and Ryder each led one of the horses towards the barn door. Madison followed them outside, until all three people and two horses stood blinking in the afternoon sun.

"Can't we just…drive?" Madison asked, hating the trepidation in her voice. She took risks, damn it, when she had the time off work. And she could be fearless — she had seven years of field hockey scars to prove it. But this horse, smallish as it had looked in the barn, seemed to grow larger the more she came to grips with the idea of actually getting on its back.

Both men looked at her, as if reassessing their original idea of just how completely and utterly unqualified for running a ranch she was.

"There aren't many…roads," Ryder said after a too-long minute, and she had to give him credit for not laughing directly in her face. Christian's nerves looked shot. "We have ATVs, if that would better?"

Out of the frying pan and into the fire.

Ryder did laugh out loud and Madison realized her face had scrunched up in distaste.

"Horses it is," Christian said, his voice tight and sharp. "I'm going to swing up first then Ryder will help

28

you, okay? Her name is Dolly and she's the sweetest horse in the barn. She won't hurt you or anything, I promise."

Ryder grinned and Christian, as he said, climbed onto the back of the horse. Madison cocked her head, watching his fluid movement.

Finally, she sighed. "The...skirt?" she asked, trying to keep her tone neutral and not at all flaming with embarrassment at her inappropriate attire for the day.

Maybe you're really embarrassed because you wouldn't mind sharing what's under your skirt with these two guys...

Ugh, no. She was just embarrassed about being a dumb city slicker, that was *all*. Nothing else. Whatever move she made from the ground to Dolly's backside, in the space behind Christian — and it definitely wouldn't be as fluid as his, would include a nice little peep show for the wildlife.

And for the two hot cowboys looking at me like I've got a second head.

"I won't tell if you won't," Ryder said with a shrug and a streak of devilry in his innocent eyes. "Just wrap your legs around Christian then tuck the fabric under. You should be okay."

There, she didn't have any more excuses, so she resigned herself to the nature of the beast. Ryder came up to her side, and she was incredibly aware of him, unable to ignore the heat or delicious scent of fresh wood, fresh air and something so masculine radiating off his large body.

Ma. Di. Son.

"All right, hold still, Ms. Hollis," he said. He wrapped his strong hands around her waist and lifted her up as if she weighed no more than a sack of potatoes. Her awareness of his strength and size increased and she had the craziest urge to press her body back against him, to take a little more of that heat and power. *Insane, for sure.*

As she was distracted, which he undoubtedly knew, Ryder slid her behind Christian's back and she gripped automatically, holding on tight. Not that that was any better than the strength behind Ryder's touch. Christian was muscled and powerful in the abdomen where she held firm, even as the horse stood still. The loose muscle tank top hanging over his body gave her a wide plain of bare skin to avoid, but there wasn't anywhere else for Madison to put her hands, so she tried not to think too much about the smooth skin below her fingers, stretching taut over hard working-man muscles. His whole body vibrated, as though he had a very thin grasp on his control. She coughed, loudly, adjusting the very little spare fabric of her skirt so it did something to cover the edges of her lace panties — a very little something, but something, nonetheless.

"So tell me about the ranch." Also too loud, followed by a too-loud squeak when Dolly took off at a leisurely pace down the dirt path and away from her car, the manor house and general signs of civilization.

"As far I as know, Triple Diamond's been in Mason's family since they moved out west, after coming here from Scotland," Ryder said, ambling along beside them on a much larger horse. It made him look like a normal-sized human, and not a cowboy carved out of a tree trunk. "They worked until they could buy up the neighboring lands and now the place covers almost three thousand acres. Those mountains" — he pointed just ahead of them, at three towering summits — "are part of the Black Reef Mountain Range. The National Parks Department cares for it, but your land stretches about halfway down that pass over there."

Madison followed his gaze, her eyes catching dazzling blues and brilliant greens and far distant trees against the mountains. It was possible she hadn't seen this much nature in her entire life combined, let alone in a single place all at one time.

"Forgive my ignorance," she said, hating it, "but how much space actually is an acre? I'd probably do a lot better with city blocks, but I've never been exposed to this kind of thing before."

To their credit, neither man commented or expressed distaste at her admission. Christian turned over his shoulder and nodded back toward the house.

"Average house in the suburbs is built on about a third of an acre. You're sitting on just under four point six square miles of land."

They had officially reached the end of the residential section of the land, the horses ambling along the dirt pathway under a clear-as-glass wide blue sky, surrounded on both sides by vast stretches of farmland.

Four point six *miles*. She owned four point six square miles of land, all designed to cultivate crops and animals. Of course, the reality of that insane truth was dwarfed by the beautiful landscape sprawling out before them, especially when the horses cleared a small section of brush and she got her first good, long look at the Black Reef Mountains.

Madison didn't have that much experience with natural mountains. San Francisco's winding, impossible geography had long been built up, torn down and built up again, but the Black Reef Mountains looked smaller than a lot of the mountain ranges she had seen in nature documentaries. It wasn't a bad thing. In fact, their accessible height and closeness to the ranch made them feel...intimate, if that was even the right way to refer to mountains. It probably wasn't.

Dolly stopped and Ryder brought his horse right up beside them, all three turning their heads to stare up at the gorgeous, sprawling landscape which seemed to stretch for miles out in every direction.

"It's...beautiful," Madison said at last, her breath catching just a little on the word. So much of her life had been spent running back and forth through the same city she had been born in. This vast natural beauty was overwhelming in so many ways all at the same time.

"It is," Ryder said, his voice not without emotion. "You can see why the Westerly Kings all stuck around." She could, though, the oddness of hearing her mother's maiden name in this sort of context added a level of unreality to the situation, and Madison blinked, trying for some purchase in the insanity.

"This is probably a lot for you to take in right now." Christian turned to face her. "You're not really a nature person, are you?"

Madison smiled. "What gave it away?" she asked, a light laugh escaping. She could swear she saw a flicker of something in his eyes, something not totally cold and distant.

"Come on, we'll take you to a private place on the ranch," Ryder replied, turning his horse to — the west? Shit, she had no clue which was west any more than she knew what sort of irrigation system was now sprinkling the crops.

"What are you guys growing this year?" Madison asked, looking at the seemingly endless stretches of dirt.

"That's all Christian's gig," Ryder said. "He's a wizard with that stuff."

Christian tensed just a little under Madison's touch, reminding her of all the very intimate places they were pressed against each other, at the thighs, at the back and belly…

"Right now we're doing legumes." Christian nodded to the field on their left. "We practice crop rotation here, because it's murder on the nutrients in the soil if you plant the same crops year after year and it keeps the bugs away. That field is peas and back there is chickpeas. They're great for in-between years because they give a lot of nutrients back to the soil instead of taking it out."

Madison smiled. She couldn't help it. The man, despite his tattoos, ripped-up tank and badass attitude, was passionate about chickpeas.

"We also don't spray," Christian continued. "Mason was real strict on that. It's risky, but it pays off on the business end, since everyone knows they're getting really safe food from Triple Diamond. We'd be shit out of luck if any of the fields got infected, but the organic pest deterrents we use here do the trick."

Madison looked out across the field, happiness rising within her, and not just because having an all-organic farm would be a great selling point. Something about this place, even in the few minutes she had been here, spoke to her on a visceral level. Knowing that their ideology for running things ran in tandem with her own was definitely an added bonus.

"We're here," Ryder said. The two horses took a slight slope and they steadied into a clearing, where a wide lake, vast and shimmering, reflected the Black Reef Mountains just beyond. A small picnic table sat near the shore, alongside one chair and a hammock tied between two trees. Other than that, she could have been looking at the scene just as Lewis and Clark had two hundred years before, all vast and expansive and completely breath-taking.

"It's a nice place to escape from everything." Christian pulled Dolly up to the water's edge then dismounted before reaching up to help her. Madison tried not to think about the way his hands felt, spanning her waist or the difference between his touch and Ryder's, and where else their touches might run different.

"We have a garden on the roof of my apartment building," Madison said a little lamely. She straightened her skirt and leaned back against a tree to look out over the water. "That's where I go to relax, whenever I get the chance. I can't really compare it to this, though, I mean, I knew the ranch had a lake, but...wow..."

Ryder lopped the two sets of horse reins over a tree branch and followed her line of vision.

"There's actually three lakes and six ponds on the property," he said, "and a river that tends to flood in the spring when the snow starts to melt in the mountains. The ponds are big, though—you might have seen the one behind Holmwood?"

She shook her head. "What's the different between a lake and pond? I thought it was size."

The grin that spread across Christian's face was sin incarnate and her nipples pebbled at the danger just below that sexy surface.

"Typical female mind, always on the size," he said, humor and heat in his dark eyes. "There's so much more to it than that..."

"Well, if you're insecure, we could certainly sit down and talk about it," Madison volleyed, before she even realized what she was doing. *Play it cool. Don't clamp your hand over your mouth. Just be cool, okay?*

Christian's eyes flashed. "I'm not insecure," he said on a low breath. "But I definitely wouldn't say no to talking about it. Or more than talking *it*."

Madison's breath hitched just a little. *He's sex on a stick and he's majorly flirting with me. Have I ever been less cool in my damn life?*

Heat sizzled and sparkled in the air and she almost lost her damn mind looking into those mysterious eyes that promised her more than she even knew how to ask for. Whatever, she was a free agent for the first time in years and there was nothing wrong at all with a little harmless flirtation, even if something deep in Christian's eyes told her that he'd take her up on the offer in a second, no questions asked...

"Christian, don't tease her," Ryder said, rolling his eyes in her direction. "He gets off on messing with people. Don't take him too seriously."

Christian leaned against the tree, all lazy control and power and intent, and raised one eyebrow with the kind of challenge that had sent stronger women into battle before.

"Or you could take me seriously," he said, letting the words linger in that in-between space of teasing and promising.

The silence stretched just a beat too long, and before Madison could ask what the *hell* had just happened, a great howl came echoing out of the woods just up the mountain range. Madison's heart froze, half in fear and half in base excitement. A wolf. A real, wild wolf—and somehow that felt even less dangerous than the two men she stood beside, both of whom seemed perfectly keen to make her howl.

"You're safe here," Ryder said, coming to stand beside her. The oddest thing was, she *felt* safe, there in those mountains, her feet upon the land where so many of her ancestors had walked. This place, a million miles away from the life she knew, didn't feel so alien as she'd thought it was going to. It felt real, hardy and safe.

None of which has anything to do with the two hot cowboys standing here flirting with you, right, Madison?

Of course not! She could look and enjoy, but that was all she planned to do. Anything more, anything that involved even tempting another response from either of them, was dangerous, forbidden territory and she should most definitely know better than to traverse it.

"There are wolves here?" she asked, hating the little squeak that followed the question because she couldn't pinpoint whether her fear came from said wolves, or from the thoughts rioting around in her head about these two very sexy, very close men. Distractions.

"We have all sorts of wildlife in these mountains," Christian replied, moving back toward where they'd tied the horses. "Wolves, raptors, bears, bobcats, coyotes, moose…"

Madison suppressed a shiver, but not very well, because Ryder rolled his eyes at Christian.

"We also have sheep, goats, deer, rabbits and a whole lot of stuff that *won't* kill you." He eyed her as Christian climbed up onto Dolly's back, then wrapped two strong hands around her waist and hoisted her up behind Christian, where she settled, surprisingly comfortable, against Christian's back. "Have you ever shot a gun, Ms. Hollis?" Ryder asked, and she didn't sense any condemnation, just a little concern at the edges of his voice. She shook her head and he shook his in turn. "If you're going to be staying out here, you're going to do well to protect yourself. We'll teach you the basics."

As they turned back toward Holmwood Manor and the main road, Madison knew just how dangerous, and tempting, a *lesson* from either of these men might be.

Chapter Four

Madison woke with the sun streaming across her face. Wait, that wasn't right. The sun was nice and warm upon her skin, but it didn't tickle, and it didn't lick her cheek with a sandpapery tongue, before slipping full on into her ear. She was groggy. The time difference between Wolf Creek and San Francisco was only an hour, but at just past five in the morning, it felt like a hell of a lot more than that.

She rubbed her eyes and tried to get her bearings. What the hell had woken her up? As far as Madison knew, she'd been imagining the weird texture against her skin. She felt under the pillow to see if maybe there was a book or something, when…

"Ouch!"

She pulled her hand free. A tiny droplet of blood pooled at the tip of her middle finger. Oh, she was wide-awake now, and she was *pissed*. She grabbed a tissue and wrapped it around her finger before yanking the pillow up to see what had stabbed her.

It was…a dust bunny? Maybe she wasn't as awake as she had thought, since dust bunnies definitely didn't bite people, and she'd never met a dust bunny that could make her bleed. Gently, she poked at it. The dust bunny unfurled into the smallest, fluffiest gray kitten Madison had ever seen.

"What are you doing in my bed?" she asked the cat, looking down at the little mop of fur, still exhausted enough that she almost expected an answer. "And why the hell did you wake me up at five o'fuck in the morning? Not all of us get to sleep in the sun all day, you know?"

The kitten smiled at her, a full-on, smug cat grin that made Madison scrunch her nose in frustration.

"That's it," she said, reaching for the kitten's scruff. "I don't know if Ryder and Christian thought they were being funny, letting you in here, but you've overstayed your welcome. I'm jetlagged and I have a long day ahead of me and it's time for you to go." She was just closing her hand around the kitten's neck when it took a flying leap, sending her careening backward into the pile of quilts at the foot of the bed.

Madison dove for it, but her foot got caught in the sheet and she lunged forward only halfway, missing the cat with her far hand and smacking her palm into the wooden headboard of the bed. So she spun out of the blankets, foot still tangled in the bottom of the sheet, and lunged for the little gray fluffball, visible mostly by his—her?—white tail and bright blue eyes. But the thing was damn quick and when Madison reached for it this time, she smacked her head against the lamp on the bedside table. It went careening to the ground, bringing a glass of water, three books and a candle in a jar of marbles smashing to the ground.

As for her, Madison had her feet and legs on the bed, even more tangled in the sheets than before, and both hands on the rug, a bit trickier now, since the marbles from the candleholder had rolled all over the floor and one misplaced hand would send her careering. From her half-crouched vantage point, the cat sat just out of reach, practically laughing. *Furry little bastard.*

She took one final lunge, lost her balance and dragged three quilts and two pillows off the bed with her, landing in a very undignified heap of bed, broken lamp, marbles and fluffy little asshole, who had just popped up onto Madison's knee and started licking her face.

And that was the moment Christian and Ryder walked into the room. And immediately lost it.

"Are you okay?" Ryder asked. The stupid dust bunny was now in her hair, knotting it as best as possible with kneading motions that were going to be a real bitch to untangle. Ryder tried, he really did. It was more than could be said for Christian, who leaned back against the door jamb and took in the whole scene in front of him, the lamp, the bed and the damn cat and grinned at her expense like it was fucking Christmas.

"I've got a bruised ego, but otherwise I'll be fine," Madison said, her voice a little bitter. "Can you take your fucking cat back, please?"

Ryder's eyes went a little wide and she realized the curse had taken him off-guard. He recovered quickly, though.

"That's not our cat," he said. "There's a litter in the barn, but I didn't bring any into the house."

Madison picked up the scruffy thing. It was soft grays and whites, with bright blue eyes and that silly little smile. *How can such a small thing cause so much chaos?*

"Well, it's an undeniable fact that there is a cat in my bedroom in your house. So what should we do about it?" The cat, apparently listening, walked from Madison's hand and into the crook of her arm, so she was resting her head against Madison's chest and shoulder.

"I think I know what the kitten wants you to do," Christian said, the amusement at her predicament never leaving his eyes. "She just wants some affection, that's all." His voice got a little colorful and passionate, just as it had when he'd spoken about the crops.

"Well, I think I'm fresh out of affection," Madison said, even as she somehow, some way, brought one hand up to the kitten's ears and stroked.

"And our work here is done," Ryder said, turning for the door. "We didn't mean to burst in like that — we just wanted to make sure you were all right. They must have heard that crash in Helena."

Madison nodded and stood from the pile of blankets, still holding the devil cat, who purred in contentment into her shoulder. "Where can I find a broom, to sweep up the broken glass?" Neither man responded. In fact, the room had gone still as a tomb, with the exception of the cat's soft breathing. "Guys?"

Christian swallowed. Hard. *Hmm, he's not exactly the kind of guy to lose his cool. What's up his ass all of a sudden?* "We're going to leave," Christian said. "Now."

And in that second, Madison realized exactly what had turned the amused, smirking men into marble statues. She had long ago taken to treating herself to expensive lingerie, well before Joshua had entered her life. The pieces weren't for anyone else as much as they were for her, frilly little indulgences that made her feel sexy and soft and happy.

And right now, standing in the guest bedroom in Ryder and Christian's house, in a slinky pale rose teddy, decorated across the top with lace trim, she felt *wanted.*

Especially since the expressions in both men's eyes were laden and overt, neither of them hiding their obvious interest. *You're not exactly hiding it either, Madison.*

"Ms. Hollis," Ryder said, in an obvious attempt to break the blanket of tension that had descended upon the room—hot, promising, making her want to succumb to all sorts of things. "Don't you know it's unkind to wear fur?"

He nodded toward the cat and Madison couldn't help it. She laughed. She laughed until the little squirt in her arms woke up and jumped onto the bed with an expression of annoyance. She laughed until even Christian's rough face held the hint of a genuine smile. She laughed until her chest hurt and she couldn't catch a deep breath.

"What the hell is happening?" Madison finally asked, sitting on the bed. She reached over to the chair near the window and snagged a sleep robe, which she tied around her, promising herself that she didn't regret covering up her body, promising herself she didn't miss their hot perusals.

"Short version, you threw a temper tantrum over a cat," Christian said. "Long version, well, I actually think I'd like to hear that story myself."

Ryder nodded in agreement.

"There's no story," Madison said, picking up the blankets and looking for shards of glass. Upon closer inspection, the lamp hadn't broken. She'd been seeing the reflections of the loose marbles from the candleholder — *thank God for small victories*. "This thing woke me up by sticking his tongue down my ear. It's four...twenty-six in San Francisco right now, so I tried to get the runt to leave. She wasn't having it."

"Like I said, temper tantrum," Christian teased. He *teased*, and not in a way that held disdain or annoyance underneath. *Oh, this is bad, this is real bad.* The expression in his eyes spoke of punishments for bad behaviors, and Madison's body grew hot in the wake of such intensity. But he didn't voice his thoughts aloud. Instead, he just continued, "We're going to make some breakfast — anything you don't like?"

Madison shook her head. "I'll eat anything. I'm not picky."

Christian laughed, a genuine laugh, and his eyes sparkled, and she knew exactly what was going through his mind, because it was going through her mind, too — would she eat anything they offered her? *I'd be more than willing to give it just a little taste...*

No. Distraction. But even after they left, taking their innuendos and wandering gazes with them, Madison had a hard time remembering why wanting these men was a bad idea.

After breakfast, she hunkered down at Ryder and Christian's kitchen table overlooking the great expanses of crops out to the west. Their home was smaller than Holmwood, but her entire apartment *building* in California would have been smaller than Holmwood, and she liked the cozy feel of the place, even with the innately male design. Still, Ryder and Christian were clean and kept house well enough for two bachelors, so she didn't have any complaints.

Well, except one tiny, teeny, little one. Being in their house, surrounded by their belongings and scents, distracted her. Big-time. Though three stacks of legal documents sat before her on the wooden table top, Madison's mind ran hot at the images of what could be done with the leather couch a room away, or whether or not the counters could hold her weight.

Her phone buzzed, another distraction from the workload.

How's the farm?

Even through text, Madison could just picture Lily's sardonic half-smile. Where Madison was definitely the city girl that Ryder and Christian seemed to think she was—if the high heels and pencil skirt hadn't been indication enough—Lily had no problem getting down and dirty. Her flower shop in downtown San Francisco had been the end result of a horticulture biology degree, and she'd spent a fair amount of time touring the wilds of California's national forests, trying to drag Madison along with her. That Madison was now the one out in the woods had been the source of endless amusement for her sister from the start.

Huge. It's beautiful out here — you should come see it before I get rid of it.

The note pinged and disappeared into the air.

Still planning to sell, then?

Yes.

Lily hadn't been subtle about her opinion that Madison should just give things a few days before delving right into unloading the place. But where Madison went by the numbers and facts and figures, Lily had always had a creative mind that saw big, exciting pictures and often meant things didn't get done. Oh, she finished projects – her own successful business was a prime example. But she'd also tried ballet, art, photography and a brief stint as an actress, so Madison usually took her first suggestion with a grain of salt.

Plus, what could she do with a ranch, after all? Triple Diamond was a massive place and she didn't even scratch the surface of the kind of knowledge needed to run it.

But you know who does know how to run a ranch?

Ugh, so not the time.

Not that there was ever a good time for her mind to take rollercoaster loops around the subject of the two hot cowboys currently working in the barn and out in the fields. While she was in here, not getting her paperwork done.

Thankfully, work had been a little lax on the amount of stuff she needed to do while on her trip. The spreadsheets were still piling up in her email inbox, but at least she wasn't responsible for any phone calls – which might have had something to do with the apologetic *I don't know how good the cell service will be out in the mountains.* She hadn't known, but, of course, that wasn't why she had said it.

Proof of a healthy working environment, Madison. Psh, nothing about working for the Silicon Valley tech titans was healthy. Those companies were constantly demanding and she tended to bear the brunt of the work at Daniels and Hark. But the job paid and it gave her a taste of what she had thought she had always wanted to do.

Except, hell, she didn't even remember why she did it most days. The joy of pulling off a great event rarely accompanied the lectures and conferences she planned and, though it paid well, San Francisco was such a wildly expensive place to live that she couldn't put much money away. Certainly not enough to make any sort of big change.

"Looks like you made a friend." Christian's voice came through the back door to the kitchen a second before he did. His hair was tied into a loose ponytail at the nape of his neck and a slight sheen of sweat covered the enticing column of his throat.

She looked at the small mop of gray fur stretched out over one stack of legal documents. A little pink Post-it note peeked out from between two kitten paws. She had tried to put the pathetic little scrap outside. This was a farm after all, and cats liked farms, didn't they? And hadn't Ryder said something about a family of kittens in the barn?

But the cat hadn't wanted to hang out outside and had made her opinion on the matter impossible to ignore by howling on just the other side of the door until Madison had been so fed up she'd let the furry brat back into the house, after damning it to hell and naming it Lucifer. Satisfied with having her demands attended to, Lucifer had given Madison a rough, sandpapery kiss before falling asleep on the table.

"I just didn't want to listen to the howling anymore," Madison said, her voice a bit tart. It wasn't the little fur ball's fault that she found herself so completely ill at ease with everything she'd worked so hard to achieve.

"Are you...are you okay?" Christian narrowed his eyes and looked at her discerningly. The change she'd seen in her bedroom that morning seemed to linger. He didn't give off an irritated or even lustful vibe, but something comfortable and easy, as though he genuinely gave a damn about her answer, despite their icy and heated exchanges. He didn't seem all that comfortable asking her about her feelings, but Madison had to admit she probably looked a sight and a half at the moment. The papers were spread around her on the desk in a haphazard mess she would never have allowed in the office and her hair had come down from its bun, spilling out over her shoulders and back in fluffy waves. Add the tension in her neck and the repeated motion of her fingers at her temples and yeah, it was pretty obvious that she fell square on the other side of okay.

"I'm fine," she said. Yeah, Christian radiated sex and temptation, but that didn't make her want to confess to all the self-doubt and frustration rioting around in her brain right now. *It's just downtime. I'm usually so busy I don't even have time to think about how fulfilled I am... I am fulfilled. Damn it, I'm fulfilled.*

"You'll forgive me for saying you don't look totally fine," he said. He rummaged around in the fridge and pulled out a pitcher, before pouring her a glass of lemonade and plunking it down on the table beside her papers. Slowly, lazily, he slid into the seat beside her. "Is it the ranch?" he asked. "Because we're going to help you with that. We care a lot about this place and we want to see it succeed."

Madison smiled and took a drink of the lemonade. To her surprise, it was...good.

"You're right." She sighed. Sure, she talked to her friends at home, to Lily, who had been first a cousin, then a sister after the accident, and always her best friend. She didn't keep her feelings bottled up.

And yet. The way Christian looked at her right then, with those heavy eyes and the slight scowl at the corner of his mouth, made her want to tell him the stuff she didn't tell anyone else, made her want to give voice to what had happened between her and Joshua, made her want to wonder, aloud, with an audience, why she continued to do a job that was driving her into ground.

But she had only met this man yesterday, and though he — and Ryder — enticed her, made her want things she hadn't given in to in a very long time, made her *want* to give in to them, it wouldn't be a wise idea to open up to him. Already Triple Diamond Ranch had a strange and unexpected hold on her, and part of her, deep down, was afraid of what that meant.

"I mean, the ranch is part of it," Madison said, despite her better judgment. "But there's more to it, too."

He nodded, understanding that she didn't want to go into the 'more to it'. A lock of hair fell over his eyes and gave him a dangerous look, one she shouldn't want to get closer to.

"There's always more to it," he said, like he knew. "Not to overstep my bounds, but I've been told I give one hell of a massage. Would that help?"

"I…I don't know if that's a good idea," Madison said after the moment had stretched between them, wide and tense. A spark of something wicked crossed those dark brown eyes, as tempting as it was challenging.

"Just to help you relax," Christian said, making an obvious effort not to smirk. "Nothing else."

Her defenses were down and she *wanted* him to touch her, wanted to feel those rough, calloused hands against her skin, against her neck. Not only was she sure it would feel damn good, but Madison knew that his touch would be the distraction she craved from the madness of everything going on in her head. So she nodded, a little tentatively, and turned her back toward him, pulling her wild hair over her shoulders so he could put his hands to her.

Christian moved, sliding his rough palms over her neck, and Madison nearly jerked out of her seat. Her skin burned hot where he had touched her, running circles of potent desire around her waist, over her shoulders, wherever he whispered his hands toward her.

Pull back, Madison. This is Bad Idea 101. Except did Bad Idea 101 include a curious questioning for how Ryder's hands would also feel on her back? Because that felt a lot more like Bad Idea, the grad program. Would giving in to flirtations with one of these sexy cowboys make her off-limits to the other? And why did it matter so much to her if it did?

"You're not relaxing," Christian whispered, his voice low and deep, just near her ear. "The point here is to help you relax." God, the husky tone of his voice made it all too clear clear that if she wanted to indulge in another kind of relaxing, he'd volunteer for the position in an instant.

"Just a lot on my mind," Madison replied honestly.

Letting him touch her was a bad idea, but she couldn't bring herself to stop it, even if this was supposed to be nothing more than a business relationship, even if she had just met him yesterday. But none of that kept her from wanting more, from needing more of his touch, of his skin, of the deep press his fingers made into the knots at her shoulders and neck. His closeness made Madison was all too aware of his strength and size. Christian emanated a lazy sort of power that had her aching behind her slack and rubbing her legs together in a desperate need for more contact, more touch.

"Would it help if I took off my blouse?" she asked. "I have a camisole underneath." It was official—she had lost her goddamn mind.

"If you'd feel comfortable, then sure," Christian replied. "Whatever helps."

And because his voice sounded just a little husky and a little wanting, a shade darker than it had before, Madison did, sliding loose each of the buttons on the front of her shirt and carefully, before she slid the silk blouse off her arms and tossed it over the chair beside her. The black camisole could hardly be considered revealing, but nonetheless she felt exposed and wicked in it, her arms and shoulders and back bare to him. *You started this, Madison. Now, you have to see it through.*

Well, from where she sat, that didn't seem like too much of a hardship.

Her breathing was shallow and Christian ground his teeth together to keep from doing something stupid, like pressing his lips to the back of her smooth neck. He could tell that Madison was engaged in some sort of internal battle about whether or not this was a good idea. He knew for a goddamn fact that it wasn't. Hell, ever since she'd sat behind him on the horse yesterday afternoon, he'd been struggling with the possessive desire to push her up against a wall and bury himself inside her. Then, seeing her in that little pink lingerie thing that morning—Jesus, it would give any man fantasies for a lifetime. Now, she sat with her bare back turned to him, awaiting his touch. His stupid idea. This whole situation could have easily been avoided, but no, he had to help a distressed-looking near stranger by offering her a *back massage*? Maybe he had fallen off too many motorcycles, like Ryder always said.

He had wanted to push her, to make her uncomfortable, to flirt and innuendo his way past those fucking high and mighty walls she'd been sporting when she'd first driven up. He liked the idea of cracking her façade, and so he'd flirted, teased, given her the look he knew women couldn't resist.

Except with his hands on her back now, Christian knew that he wasn't being entirely honest with himself. Deep down, part of him had been flirting with this woman for real, because she made him burn, deep and low, made him want to do something wild and stupid, made him want to do *her*. He'd thought she would crack, but she hadn't. She hadn't bowed or kowtowed. She'd parried his remarks right back to him and she'd done it well. He had to give her that, even though there was a whole hell of a lot more he wanted to give her.

He brushed one more strand of her hair over her shoulders and paused mid-motion. And *fuck*, because this woman, despite the high heels and the city girl attitude and the fear of horses and kittens, turned him on like no one ever had. Especially since a little sliver of lacy purple bra peeked out from behind her black tank top and just below it was a tattoo…

In an instant, Christian's mind conjured a thousand images of Madison Hollis wearing nothing at all but that tattoo and whatever other surprises she had hiding across her skin.

"You don't strike me as the tattoo kind," Christian said, sinking his thumbs into the tight knots at her shoulders and kneading just that little bit.

Madison arched into his touch and he liked the motion way too much for what this was supposed to be — an innocent, helpful way to relieve stress.

"You barely know me," she said, her voice light and a little teasing. She didn't quite strike him as the teasing kind, either, but she was right — he *didn't* know her, despite the undercurrent of connection that made him want to meet her intimately on a whole lot of levels.

"So, tell me something about you," he replied, sliding his hands down her back, maybe just a little inappropriately and seemingly unable to stop himself. Yeah, he wanted her. He wanted her bad. "What's the tattoo for?" The piece was beautiful, delicate but still powerful, just like the woman who wore it. It was a small, intricately patterned monkey in a tree, done in the watercolor style of tattooing that could either go really well or really badly. In her case, it looked incredible and he felt the insane urge to lick her skin below the colored ink.

"My parents used to call me monkey," she said, her voice a little far off and a little distant and a little sad.

"Used to?"

Madison turned around and faced him, her eyes dry but stained with memories. "They died when I was ten," she said. "My uncle and aunt adopted me."

Without meaning to, Christian reached out and took her hand in his much larger one, guilt streaking across his mind. He knew better than to judge people, given all he'd been judged for his whole life, and yet he'd reacted to her presence without a second thought and he'd made some mistakes.

"I'm sorry," he said, his voice low, meaning it for more reasons than one.

She looked away but didn't move her hand. "It was a long time ago," she said. "I'm okay."

"You can still be sad," Christian replied. "My mom died when I was fourteen. It's kind of how Ryder and I got so close, actually. It's been a long time, but I still miss her. I won't ever not."

She nodded and he was pleased to see her accepting the empathy. Madison Hollis didn't seem like the kind of person who accepted help from anyone, and certainly not pity. He would know. He'd been the exact same way when his mom had died. He'd shut out the world, daring them to come fuck with him. And, thankfully, Ryder Dean had done just that, worming his way into Christian's life with a badass attitude that had gotten them in trouble for over fifteen years.

"Of course not," she said. "And I'm sorry that happened to you, too. But you're lucky you had Ryder. I don't know how I would have survived without my cousin Lily. She's my everything."

"She sounds great," Christian said. He stood up, mostly because his feet were growing a little jittery and his breathing a little rough. It had been years since he'd talked about his mom and the fact that this woman he had just met pulled some strange desire to do just that out of him — well, he didn't really like it all that much.

At that moment, the back door to the kitchen swung open and Ryder walked into the kitchen, shirtless as usual.

"Why the long faces?" he asked plopping a box on the counter and indicating the cat asleep on Ms. Hollis' notes. "I thought you might want this."

Madison scowled. "She's going back to the barn. I only let her in because she wouldn't stop yelling. Awful loud for being such a little thing."

Ryder raised an eyebrow and Christian just laughed, though his mind whirled in the direction of exactly how *loud* Madison would be.

"Hey." She narrowed her eyes, but he glimpsed a spark of desire in the dark, condemning gaze. "Whatever you're thinking right about now, stop it. Both of you. I'm not a cat." And she wasn't exactly a *little* thing, either. She was tall and curvy, with an ass that filled out a pair of dress pants and a tight, thin skirt with equal skill. Not that Christian had been watching, because he definitely hadn't. Flirting to make a point, not for any other reason. *Yeah right.*

"Yes ma'am," Ryder said. He put the box on the ground and grabbed a beer from the fridge. "Have you named it yet? Or are you just going to keep calling it cat?"

"Very Holly Golightly. And I'm thinking Lucy." She smiled up at both of them with an expression of innocence so sincere that it took Christian a moment to comprehend what she said next. "Short for Lucifer."

The cat—Lucy—stood up from Madison's pile of books and stretched. Then, seeming to keep eye contact with Madison, it swatted at a stack of papers until the entire pile careened to the floor.

Madison gave them a fake grin. "Isn't she just the cutest?"

"It's your warm welcome," Christian said, looking down at the cat.

"Oh, speaking of," he continued, accepting the beer Ryder handed him without him asking. "We meant to tell you yesterday, but you passed out. There's something you should see. It's over at Holmwood, if you want to take a break." The expression on her face said she'd be interested in taking the kind of break that had nothing to do with the old manor house except the beds they'd find inside, but she squared her shoulders and grappled for control. Christian couldn't help but wonder what she'd be like if she gave it up.

They walked through the unlocked back door to Holmwood — *ha, would I ever leave the back door to my apartment unlocked?* — and though Madison had tried to insist she had work to do, both men eyed her with such discerning and, admittedly, unsettling gazes that she gave up her weak protestations and followed them…where?

Was it a good idea for her to be walking with two strange men through the hallways of a house she had never been in before? Was it a good idea for her to feel like Ryder and Christian weren't actually strangers, but two men who, despite having only just met her, seemed to have a much deeper impact on her psyche than anyone else she had only ever spent two days with? She could for sure answer that question. No, it was not a good idea.

They walked up a flight of stairs and down a hallway until they stopped before a door. Ryder fished a set of keys from his low-slung jeans and Madison tried not to look. She really did. But she couldn't deny the firm, hard muscles stretching from shoulder to waist, accentuating a deep summertime tan across broad, powerful biceps. Her defenses were down and she was acutely aware of Christian leaning against the doorframe just behind her, a powerful, overwhelming force that was just as distracting, and delectable, as

Ryder's chiseled back. *Stupid man, can't even put on a stupid T-shirt.*

He unlocked the door and motioned for her to go into the massive room. It was obviously the master bedroom—the space was twice the size of her very expensive San Francisco apartment. It smelled of rich, fresh wood and the lingering breeze from the warm summer afternoon lapping at a shuddering windowpane.

"In here, Ms. Hollis," Ryder said. He placed his hand gently around her waist to guide her through a small doorway and released his touch in an instant. Her skin burned where his fingers had been, but she tried not to react and instead followed the two men, and Lucy, her ass high in the air, into a small closet—if walk-in closets could ever be called small. In San Fran, they passed for apartments.

Ryder buried his head in a shelf and Christian closed the small closet entryway off with the bulk of his body, leaning against the door jamb. Christ, the man was big. A black tank top hung low off his muscled, powerful frame and he had at least a head on her. The idea of that much muscle and power and want...

No. You're losing your cool, Madison. The inheritance, Joshua, it all has your defenses down.

"Here it is," Ryder said. He pulled a box down from a high shelf, knocking a sweater onto the kitten in the process, who voiced her obvious displeasure. Though the room smelled faintly of mothballs, there weren't any dust or cobwebs on the box. In fact, despite being shoved to the back of the closet, it looked well cared for. "Mason showed us these pictures a few times over the years. He never said why your family stayed away, but I think he really regretted whatever caused the rift."

Madison accepted the box and lifted the lid cautiously. She almost dropped it. There, right on the very top of a stack of photos, was a picture of her mother sitting under the maple tree right outside Holmwood Manor. The tree had been smaller back then, and her mother couldn't have been more than twelve or fourteen, but there was no mistaking her. The reminder of her mother's perpetual smile and the softness of her cheeks, along with the confusion of seeing it *there* had Madison shutting the box closed tight. She needed privacy and a lot less distraction to look at these photos.

"Is it all right if I look through these on my own?" she asked. "Can I take them out of this room?"

Ryder's smile was a little sad. "It's your ranch," he said. "You can do whatever you want."

The heated tone of his drawl pulled her back to the present, kindling an undeniable awareness of the two hulking cowboys in the very small closet. God damn it, it *was* her ranch. And it had been one hell of a week, between the shattering and overdue breakup with Joshua, who'd sought greener pastures, and the reality of her family's ghosts coming into stark focus.

Maybe it wasn't such a bad idea to let go, to give in to something she wanted. She worked too damn hard to have not enough fun, and it turned out that some people weren't worth waiting around for, anyway. She should make the best of this little adventure, sow her wild oats and enjoy herself. She had no doubt that there were two willing participants in the room with her right now. And with her disastrous relationship at an end, she had two years of flirting to catch up on.

"*Whatever* I want?" The words spilled out before she thought better of it. But Madison refused to regret it. No, she was going to let loose for a change.

Christian's lazy, deliberate pose against the doorframe grew even more pronounced and intentional. She couldn't walk through the door without touching him, and Ryder leaned back on the shelf in the very small space, nearly pressing himself against her back.

"Well, city girl," Ryder drawled low, intent apparent in those few and challenging words, "that depends on what you want to do."

Chapter Five

Maybe he was pushing her. But the woman standing before him in Mason's old closet, with her tight dress pants and fuck-me high heels, didn't look like the sort of person who cowered easily. Plus, he hadn't missed the radiating heat or the intense perusal she'd given both him and Christian since driving up in that fool white BMW yesterday. Judging by Christian's expression, he was just as aware of Ms. Hollis' wandering lust. And Christian was reacting—his best friend of twenty years reacted by acting out, being over the top flirtatious, pushing buttons, stepping on toes. From the second Christian had spoken to her, Ryder knew she was under his skin.

But damn it to hell, this woman was getting under Ryder's skin, too. Ever since she had arrived, stepping out of that damn sports car in shoes meant for the runway, he'd thought of little else other than stripping her down and pressing her against the nearest flat surface—and he wasn't the only one. He'd seen that look in Christian's eyes enough times to know exactly what his best friend was thinking, and it ran something similar to his own depraved fantasies. Sure, Christian could be a bitch about it. They'd both been rocked a little on their heels by expecting some white-haired old man for an owner and getting the stuff of nighttime fantasies instead. But where Christian poked and prodded, Ryder let it roll off his back, indulging in a little of the daytime fantasies that went along with her ass in those tight dress pants. He'd been dealt some hard hands in his life, and there were things a hell of a lot worse than coming to the unnecessary rescue of a woman in pink lingerie, especially a woman who looked like her.

For once, a tiny, hidden part of him surged at the idea of having Madison Hollis all to himself. He and Christian had always been open about this particular kink—it worked for them and the women they were with seemed to enjoy it very much. But this particular woman called to him on a deeper, more carnal level than anyone he'd been with, alone or with Christian, in the past. And Jesus, she'd been here a day. *Fucking dangerous.*

She looked up at him challengingly, and she needed to look up. Though curvy at the generous breasts and hips, she was overall a slight thing, which had Ryder wondering right away about how tight she might feel wrapping her legs around his waist as he drove hard into her heat. A *totally* normal reaction to just meeting a person. The slight pout of her full pink lips didn't help his hardening cock any.

She was made intimately aware of that fact when she leaned back just a little, rubbing that totally insane ass against the front of his jeans. Her gaze flashed when she brushed his growing erection, arguably a second longer than necessary, before walking free of the closet. She strode out of the bedroom door, the tall, thin heels making her ass sway until Ryder's mind burned, then she tossed a deliberate look over her shoulder.

"I want a drink," she said.

* * * *

An hour later, Christian sat at the picnic table and looked out over the lake. Ryder stood at the grill and the familiar smell of burgers and toasting buns brought back a flood of memories, years of early summer nights just like this one. Christian felt the pang of Mason's loss all over again, making him itchy and uncomfortable.

"I'm going to miss this," he said low, not sure if his friend had heard him over the sizzle of meat. Back still turned his way, Ryder nodded.

"It's not a done deal, man," he said, "but I know. I miss Mason." His voice got a little scruffy, which always meant Ryder was feeling an emotion. Christian had known the guy long enough not to press. If Ryder wanted to talk, he would.

"She seems pretty intent on selling the place. Think she'll change her mind after looking through those photos?" Christian didn't want to get his hopes up, but there had been so few things in his life to be really hopeful for.

"Maybe." Ryder shrugged and glanced over to the back door of their house before turning around to face him. Ms. Hollis was up in their guest bedroom right now, grabbing a quick shower before she'd promised to come meet them for dinner. Images of her under the spray, body soapy and glistening, got him hard in a breath.

"We're three weeks short," Ryder said, his expression promising trouble of one kind or another. "Mason put it in the will. There's got to be a way for us to get that money, a loan or something."

Christian looked down the narrow neck of his beer bottle. He owned a couple of things that could serve as bank collateral, a few collectibles Mason had given him over the years, a high tech computer that he'd purchased after getting his degree, his custom Harley. It was worth considering — assuming the written clause was legal and not just a gentlemen's agreement. He nearly scoffed at that. No one would ever call him — or Ryder, or *Mason* — a gentleman.

"*If* it's legal," Christian put in. "You're assuming a lot there." Still, something a hell of a lot like hope glowed in his chest.

"She'll want to sell it to us," Ryder replied, his voice confident. "Hell, she'll be happy to. It gives us the responsibility and she just gets paid for a chunk of the land. It's not a bad deal."

Christian raised an eyebrow, but Ryder did have a point. "How quickly can we get that kind of money together, though?" he asked. The ranch was big enough to need an office manager and payroll was still going through, but it would take almost a month of that income to square off their required 'family rate' to buy the section of ranch Mason had once promised them. They needed another way to get it.

"A few days," Ryder said. "I can go to the bank tomorrow and figure out the details."

"And the city girl?" Christian asked. The damn city girl who'd been plaguing his mind with delicious sinful images of pencil skirts and red high heels. He didn't want to want her, didn't want there to be anything below the sinful banter and laced innuendo they'd shared. But, of course, he did — want her, that was. The way she gave as good as she got, and how she seemed to be taken in by Triple Diamond, was getting to him. And that really pissed him off.

"I mean…" Ryder paused, an almost guilty expression on his face. "We could keep her busy, ya know? I'm not the only one getting those vibes, am I?"

Christian raised an eyebrow, a small smile tugging at his lips. Despite his hedonistic tendencies, Ryder played that choirboy innocence to the very end.

"Are you suggesting…" he began, knowing full well what Ryder was suggesting, but wanting it said out loud, wanting to be certain they were on the exact same page.

"A fling," Ryder clarified. "Nothing we've never done before, and she's one hell of a flirt. It'll keep her distracted from the sales documents for a few days while we square things off at the bank."

"So, we sleep with her for long enough to get the loan?" Christian asked.

Ryder made a face. "Don't be crude. We both want her and she clearly wants us. It doesn't make sense to tell her about the deal with Mason until we know for certain we can afford it. How about we give her the…tour of Wolf Creek and we can tell her the truth when we know the score? How's that sound?"

Christian shrugged. He didn't love the idea of keeping the truth from her, stupid as it was that he felt anything for this woman but patent dislike. Still, there wasn't any point to telling her before they knew all the facts. And as for the seducing part, well, if she was game, so was he, and by the expressions she'd been throwing in both their directions today, she was definitely ready. His cock gave a mighty pulse.

"I'm in." He lifted the beer bottle to his lips just as the back door swung open and Madison Hollis stepped out. She had forgone the professional attire and slipped into a sunny summer dress with a pair of thick sandals on her feet. Better than the high heels, but still not ranch attire. Though the soft cotton flowed, the dress accentuated her enticing breasts, straining over the neckline. It cinched at the waist, making Christian ache to put his hands there.

"You'll forgive me for saying this, but you look mighty country right now, Ms. Hollis," Ryder said. *Damn, that boy can lay an accent on with a shovel.*

"You can call me Madison," she said, stepping down the stairs to join them on the patio, the little gray kitten that had been stalking her all day weaving around her feet. Christian grabbed a beer from the cooler, popped off the top and handed it to her. She smiled and, when she put the drink to her lips, her throat bobbed and dipped, bringing to mind all sorts of carnal images of what else she might be interested in swallowing.

"Well, then you have to call me Ryder," Ry replied, "and call him Chris."

Christian growled. "Please don't call me Chris," he said. "I hate that name."

Madison settled into the seat across from him at the table and laughed. She had a nice laugh, even if it did sound a little underused.

"I know what you mean. People always try to give me nicknames and none of them ever stick. My cousin calls me Mads, but she's the only one."

Christian raked his hand through his hair. It was long enough to tie up now, but he liked it at this length and it gave him something to do with his hands.

"I think you'd make a good Maddy," he said. "It's sweeter." *Where the fuck did that come from?*

"You think I'm sweet?" It was a challenge. Yeah, there was a reason he liked her, despite everything.

Christian put the beer bottle to his lips and took a very long drink.

"I think you've been playing tough city girl for a long time and you'd like to be sweet," he said. Then he leaned down, cutting the space between them in half. "Don't you like the idea of someone taking care of you for a change?"

Most women would have been cowed by a question like that, but Ms. Madison Hollis had his number in an instant. He liked that.

"Of course not," she said, more of that light laugh following. "I enjoy being in control."

Ryder leaned back against the side of the house and gave her his infamous smile.

"Of everything?" he asked.

She wanted to bristle, anyone could tell, but the city girl had backbone and she shot him a dazzling, winning smile, instead.

"Are you offering to do my expense reports for me?" she asked. "Because I could definitely part with those."

Christian laughed and raised his beer. "Nice shot." Ryder just grumbled and went back to the grill.

"So, what do you do for work?" Christian asked.

"Event management," she replied. "I organize parties and conferences for the tech companies in Silicon Valley." She called over to Ryder, "So, those expense reports are a real bitch!"

Christian just laughed and, to his surprise, it was genuine. Fine, maybe he had judged her a little too harshly in the beginning. *So what?*

"It sounds like interesting work. You like it?"

Madison leaned her head back and looked up at the sky. It was just starting to fade to evening, a handful of stars peeking out from the streaked-blue sunset.

"I always wanted to go into event planning, but I guess I didn't think it'd be like this. I'd like it more if I ever got a break," she said. "I'm all about hard work, don't get me wrong, but I'm up to eighty hours a week now and you won't believe the mountains I had to move to get a few days off to come here. If things hadn't been sour before, I'd almost understand why Josh..." She froze and suddenly became very interested in the label on her beer bottle.

"Sounds like there's a story there," Ryder said, bringing over a plate of hot burgers. "Wanna unload on a couple strangers?"

She looked up, but her smile was sadder this time and that pissed Christian off. Ryder would say he was a softy, but he just really hated the idea of seeing that look in anyone's eyes and, though Madison Hollis had only been in his life for two days, he felt a certain connection he couldn't quite explain, despite wishing he didn't.

"This old sob story?" Her laugh was humorless. "I'm good, thanks."

"Another beer?" Christian asked, opening one before she could reply and her smile morphed into something more genuine.

"That I will take you up on."

The subject was dropped, but they traded amiable conversation about the ranch and her job. She asked them about their degrees and why they'd gone into the fields they had, and they told her about her uncle, about the wild, caring man he had been throughout their whole lives. It was an easy and comfortable. In fact, despite her high-heeled entrance, Christian liked the city girl. The trick was going to be not liking her too much.

Madison was in trouble. With a double major in college then a high-profile job, she wasn't usually the one in trouble. She was usually the one with her head buried in the books or working late into the night. But with a cold beer pressed against her lips and the soft sounds of the farm life around them and the gorgeous, enticing, *tempting* company, she was definitely in danger here.

Spending time with Ryder Dean and Christian Harlow was *easy*. Too easy. Easy in a way it hadn't been with Joshua since the very beginning. If she didn't get her head on straight, they were going to notice how distracted she was. Selling the ranch was supposed to be a simple business transaction, but from the moment she had set foot on Triple Diamond and spied the two ranch managers leaning against the fence like sin incarnate, the situation had become something else entirely.

And that meant trouble. Sure, she had given herself permission to flirt and play, but the very real truth was that she wanted them. *Both* of them. And what kind of weirdo freak did that make her? Yet another thing Joshua had dropped onto the laundry list throughout their too-long relationship. He had been a missionary man all the way — except when it came to the good Lord's blessing about monogamy, apparently.

But none of that, not the ranch deal, nor Joshua, nor work, changed Madison's deep ache to touch, to explore the cords of muscle and straining power of these two wild men — and she had no doubt they'd be wild and uninhibited, capable of giving her what she needed most. But how did she go about broaching *that* subject? She couldn't just say *hey, my ex was a shithead, I'm a workaholic and how do you feel about a threesome?* They already thought she was a bit off her rocker because of those damn high heels — no need to make things weirder.

"You're thinking so hard, you'll snap that beer bottle in half, city girl," Christian said, his tone full of swagger and heat, smoldering and intense. She felt more comfortable around him than Ryder, even with the innuendos and the back massages and the dark expressions hidden in his gaze. Christian, she understood. He was the biker, the rebel, the long-haired, tattooed one. Christian made sense. Even the barbed and over the top flirtation was part and parcel of his image. He hadn't wanted her here and she could appreciate that. She hadn't wanted her here, either. But Ryder, well, something simmered just below his pretty boy surface that was both intriguing and a little dangerous.

"I wasn't…" she said, trying to discreetly unclench her fingers from the bottle. Christian curled his mouth into a knowing smirk and heat pooled deep in her belly from that single loaded look. She should play it safe, say her goodnights and remove herself from temptation.

But what about taking life by the horns? What about disproving everything Joshua said about me being married to my job? Everything in my life has already been turned on its head – what the hell is so wrong with giving in to the crazy? What about having a fling and not giving a damn about the consequences? Yeah. What about it?

"How cold is the lake?" she asked, not giving herself the chance to back down. She was out in the middle of Nowheresville, Montana, and she was damn well going to enjoy herself.

"It's cold," Ryder said, the expression in his eyes anything but. "Though if you move around a little, I'm sure you could find some way to keep warm."

There was no mistaking the innuendo in his tone or the heat in his gaze that promised he would do a *damn* fine job of keeping her warm. *Well, regrets are for tomorrow, right?*

Instead of replying, Madison unlaced her high wedges and put them onto the bench. Then she stood up, gave both men her most winning smile and turned toward the lake.

"Last one in cleans up dinner," she shouted and took off for the water.

The men were fast. She hadn't gone more than five strides when strong arms caught her by the waist and lifted her up off the ground.

"You play dirty, city girl," Ryder whispered in her ear. Out of pure instinct, she arched her back, aching to get closer to the heat and lust emanating from his big body.

"What are you going to do about it?" she challenged. *Ha, if the team at work could see me now.*

"Oh, I have a few ideas," Ryder replied, his mouth closer now, so damn close that if she just looked up she could…

Splash.

That son of a bitch... The water really was cold, but Madison barely felt it against the heat of her skin in the wake of Ryder's touch, lust warming her blood and pooling in her belly. He wanted her too, if the press of his hard cock against her back had been any indication. The only question was, what about Christian?

Greedy, Madison?

I'll never get this chance again and I'm damn well taking it.

She stayed under the water for a moment, trying to calm her racing lust. Then she made her way to the surface, pushing soaked hair out of her eyes and trying to ignore the muck under her feet. Christian sat on the shore, pulling off his large biker boots. Ryder had taken off his shirt—again—and stood like some vision in streaks of early moonlight and bright summer-blue sky that had her aching...for *something*.

"That was quite a hello, welcome to the neighborhood," Madison said, putting her hands on her hips. "Aren't cowboys supposed to have a sense of honor or something?"

Ryder scoffed and somehow even that was sexy. "If you come a little closer, I'd be more than happy to give you a *hello, welcome to the neighborhood*," he said, so much intent lacing his words that Madison's breath caught. "And forget manners. The only thing you gotta know about cowboys is that they're *real* good at riding."

She moaned, a real, audible moan, and both men froze in place.

"Maddy, if you make that sound again, I'm not going to content myself with just enjoying the view," Christian growled.

She glanced down, only to realize that her dress had soaked transparent, exposing two very peaked nipples through the soft cotton. It was now or never, then.

"Well, what *are* you going to do?" she asked.

Some of the hesitation must have slipped into her voice, because they both became instantly serious.

"Nothing you don't want," Ryder said. "But *anything* you do..." Damn, that made her all kinds of hot and bothered.

"So, how does this work then?" Madison asked. "You two go around propositioning women all the time? Or maybe one of you just really likes to watch?"

Humor sparkled in the men's eyes.

"Not all the time," Ryder said. "Only for very special women."

Madison raised an eyebrow. "Even city girls?"

"You'd be our first city girl," Christian said. "Think you're up to the challenge?"

Maddy grinned and stepped back when both men approached the water's edge.

"Why don't you come and get me, then we'll see?" she challenged, diving under the cold water. Damn, but she liked being bold. Especially since being bold meant that two incredibly hot cowboys were following her into the water right now.

A hand wrapped around her ankle, tugging her to the surface and, when Madison came up, she wrapped her legs around Ryder's waist. Jesus, that man had a body like a fucking Greek god and now she finally got the chance to touch.

"Well," she said, giving him a cheeky smile. Christian started running his hands down her sides and back with all sorts of promises. "Now that you've got me, gentlemen, what are you going to do with me?"

Ryder's grin was wolfish and, despite the coolness of the lake, her whole body ran with heat and anticipation. Joshua hadn't inspired such a carnal reaction from her in months, and all this stranger had to do was smile?

And press his large cock into her hip.

"That depends entirely on what you want." Christian's breath was hot and promising upon her neck as he spoke, barely a whisper, a not-yet touch both maddening and decadent at once. She leaned her head back against his broad chest, enjoying the press of muscles. These men didn't sit behind desks crunching numbers and building phone apps. These men worked the land, raised animals, grew food. Their muscles didn't come from hours in the gym, but days spent out in the fields doing honest, hard work. Fuck if some deep-rooted cavewoman part of herself didn't find that idea immensely arousing.

"Tell us, Maddy," he said, the words a demand, not a request, and her nipples pebbled to hard points at his predatory tone. "Tell us what you want and we'll give it to you."

What I want. What do I want?

Madison faltered, just for a second. Did she really think she was the kind of woman who could just go along with something like this, just give in to her desires and take what she wanted? *Ha. I'm starting to sound like Joshua. No, fuck that. Tonight is all about taking exactly what I want.*

"Kiss me," she said, her voice bold in the night air. Above her, bright pinpricks of stars pierced the sapphire-blue sky. There were never any stars in the city and that made her feel a little wanton and a little natural and a little base—or maybe it was just the sensation of being sandwiched between two drop-dead-sexy cowboys that had her feeling that way.

"Kiss me," she said again. This time, there was no moment of pause, no chance to regret her words, because Ryder's mouth came down upon her, hot and heavy and demanding. Their lips met and she groaned at the connection, registering how both of their cocks surged against her at the sound. Ryder coaxed her lips open, sneaking his tongue between her lips and exploring her mouth, and Christian placed wicked, promising kisses to the back of her neck and down her collarbone. He paused to nip, his teeth sharp, and she bucked against him, never breaking the connection with Ryder.

"Slow down, city girl," Christian said, his voice an octave lower than before. "We have all night to make you scream. There's no rush." His words were hot and potent — and wrong. Because the need to touch, to give in to her base lust, climbed up Madison's spine like a wildfire breaking, setting her mind and body aflame. She didn't have all night. She needed this now — she needed *them*.

Ryder stroked her peaked nipple through the soaked fabric then lowered his head to suck her into his mouth, sending a zing of electric pleasure pulsing through her. She pressed back against Christian's hardening erection and the ache between her legs bloomed into something no longer under her control.

"Come on." Ryder lifted her higher on his waist and walked to the shore. "I want you where I can see you, all spread out and taking my cock."

Madison moaned. Out loud. And judging by the expression on both their faces, it had been *very* loud.

Ryder placed her down on the picnic table and hovered just out of reach, his eyes hooded and his gaze intense.

"You're about to snap, aren't you, sugar?" It wasn't a question. The cowboy drawl was much more pronounced when he was aroused and heat pooled low in Madison's belly, her need to be filled mounting with every promising word.

"Please…" She didn't even know what she was begging for, but *Jesus,* two gorgeous men just loomed over her, half-bare, water dripping from their muscles.

"What do you think, Ry?' Christian said, though he looked straight at her. "Should we give the city girl what she wants?" He bit his lower lip just a little. "What she *needs*?"

Madison grabbed his hand and pulled him down to her, joining their mouths in a searing kiss. The men kissed in different ways. Where Ryder was a blaze, burning up the countryside with abandon, kissing Christian was like being on the back of a motorcycle, taking the corners too fast. She moaned against his mouth and he rocked into her.

"It's sexy as hell when you moan," Ryder murmured, his tone husky with want. For her. *Fuck, that's a heady feeling.* "Put your feet on the table, sugar." The word sounded raw and rebellious, torn from his lips. So, she did as she was told, placing her bare feet on the table as she continued kissing Christian. His wandering hands skirted the tips of her swollen nipples and she arched, lifting off the table to get more of his taste and his touch.

Then Ryder's hands slid up her legs, warm and muscled and with each touch her heat quickened and her breath caught. With his hands under her knees, Ryder spread her legs wider, putting her on display for his perusal, something that should have flat-out embarrassed her, but instead made her pussy wet as hell, even more so when Ryder slid one finger up her slit. She was still covered by the lace panties she had soaked in the lake but which were now wet for another reason altogether.

"I like the lace," he murmured. "But it's just so proper and I want to see all of you." The words were hot and heavy and he pressed his mouth to the inside of her thigh. "I wanna taste you."

Madison managed to break away from Christian's kiss long enough to whisper, "Then taste me."

Ryder grinned up at her and removed her panties in a long, slow, deliberation action, tossing them to the ground. Then she really was bare, totally exposed and hot and wet and needing his touch — both their touches — like she needed her next breath.

"She's so wet, Christian," Ryder murmured, his tone almost reverent. "I bet you could take my cock right now, sugar."

Damn, that sounded like a good idea to her. She needed more than this teasing and toying, so she ran her hand up Christian's wet jeans, cupping his hardness behind the fabric before reaching up to the fly, then she slid his zipper down and stroked him, aching to feel him inside her at the same time as she felt Ryder.

"Take it out," she demanded.

Christian's eyes glistened, his gaze as predatory as a wild jaguar, but he did as he was told and slowly pushed his jeans down. Even from behind his briefs, Christian's thick erection throbbed and she ached for it.

"I want you," she murmured to him, while Ryder distracted her with small but potent kisses up the soft flesh of her inner thigh. Fuck, but that man was toying with her. They both were.

Christian pulled his cock free and it jutted forth from a nest of dark curls. Madison licked her lips and sighed, low and heated.

"Don't make those sounds if you're not ready to deal with the consequences," Christian murmured. "I could get off just listening to you moan."

"Or you could get off in my mouth," she said, giving in to her uncharacteristic boldness of the evening. "Will you?"

He leaned in toward her, bringing his cock, close but not close enough for Madison to taste him like she so wanted to do.

"You have to ask me properly," he said. "I want to hear how much you want it."

These men and their filthy words might just kill her. *But what a way to go.*

She pursed her lips. "Please?"

Christian stroked his cock, just out of reach, a wicked smirk on his kiss-swollen lips. "You're going to have to try harder than that," he said.

"Please can I suck your cock?"

He grinned, but the thin veil of self-control holding him together frayed before her eyes.

"Since you asked so nicely," he said. Then he slid the plump head of his cock across her lips, the salty, masculine taste heady and seductive, and Madison darted out her tongue and licked the tip.

He hissed. "Tease."

Before she could reply, Ryder pressed a kiss to her wet hole and she bucked off the table in an instant. Two pairs of strong hands came to her hips, steadying her, holding her down to withstand the pleasurable torture.

But before Ryder could distract her any more, Madison wrapped her lips around Christian's head, sucking him into her mouth and enjoying the weight of him across her tongue. Ryder continued his teasing licks on her entrance, sucking and tempting until Madison thought she might just explode right then and there.

Then he slipped one finger between her swollen pussy folds and pumped it with slow deliberation in and out of her wanting body, both men holding her firm so she couldn't press against his touch, needing more delicious friction. Ryder added another finger and Madison's body burned with the telltale rise of her release, building between her legs and racing up her spine. Christian's cock in her mouth made her all the hotter and she sucked him deep at the exact moment Ryder brushed his rough thumb over her clit.

She hummed her pleasure around Christian's cock and he slid his hands into her hair, pulling the strands he grasped tight. The spark of pain was bare and delicious.

"That's right, baby," Christian said, "you like sucking cock, don't you?"

She really, really did, and she moaned around his thick length, relaxing her throat to take him even deeper. "Fuck, that's good, *so good...*" Christian mumbled and cursed and she took no small amount of pride in that.

But then Ryder dropped to his knees before her pussy and slid his tongue across her. He slipped inside and, *oh, fuck* she broke. Without warning, she came, hard, the force of her release crashing through her like an explosion. She rocked against his mouth, against his touch, taking Christian's cock even deeper when she rode the tremors of pleasure until both of them steadied her against the table as she came down from her intense release.

"Fuck, that was so hot…" Christian groaned. "You all right?" All right—she'd just had the most insane orgasm of her life and they were asking if she was *all right*? In response, she sucked his cock to the back of her throat and worked her hand up and down his thick shaft.

"I wanna fuck your tight hole and feel you come all over my cock," Ryder said, his voice rough. "Do you want that, Madison?"

Oh, *hell* yes, she wanted that. She nodded around Christian's cock and tightened her cheeks at his reaction. He was losing control and she tempered her wild movements, swallowing him down hard until he was mumbling out a string of curse words and holding her head steady around his cock.

"Fuck, baby, I'm going to come…"

She kept her mouth wrapped around him even as he tried to pull away and a moment later he shot thick strands of cum, hot and salty against her tongue. Spent and breathing hard, he pulled back and collapsed against the picnic table bench.

"You might have killed him," Ryder said with a laugh that could have been a groan. "I can't wait to see what you do to me."

Eyes heavy and breathing shallow, another orgasm already on the horizon, Madison managed to challenge, "Then what are you waiting for?"

Ryder reacted in an instant, his body going rigid and his eyes growing even hotter with need and desperation. He turned around, grabbed his wallet off a chair and dug out a foil-wrapped condom. He shucked off his wet jeans, his hard lines of muscle shimmering in the bright moonlight. *Fuck, this guy is full-on cowboy porn.* She had cowboy porn and biker porn — right then, nothing was wrong with life.

Ryder gave his thick cock a stroke, the sight so hot and mesmerizing that Madison ached to have him deep inside her. *God, what if they both want to fuck me at once...No...*

"Do you want us to?" Christian asked. *Shit,* had she said that out loud?

Normally, she would have blushed. Hell, normally she wouldn't have even thought something so outright insane, let alone *said* the damn thing out loud. But *normally* had gone out of the window when she'd propositioned the two hot ranch managers to fuck her on a picnic table. So no blushing, not this time. This time she reached her hand up her body and plucked at her swollen nipple, her eyes trained on Christian the whole time. Already, his cock swelled to life again, and she wondered how long it would take him to be ready for her.

Ryder slipped a finger into her slick entrance, then another, sliding them thick against her pussy walls, and she clenched him. Hard.

"Fuck, that's tight, sugar." He pushed in a third finger and her whole body bowed at the sensation of being stretched. *Ha, barely.* When Madison glanced down the table, she got a view of the full, rigid erection that had pressed against her in the lake. Yeah, she had no idea what being *stretched* meant. Yet. Ryder must have sensed her hesitation, because he stopped teasing her in an instant.

"Everything okay?" he asked, concern evident in his voice.

Madison let out a soft groan, her mind not quite able to keep up with everything her body wanted with such desperation. "I don't know how you're going to fit," she admitted, even though her desire mounted by the heavily charged second.

"Baby, you're so slick I think we could both fit in you right now," Ryder said on a strained laugh. "How about I go slow, and if you need me to stop, just say the word."

She nodded, her brain fuzzy with heat and desire and the way Ryder's cock felt nudging against her swollen entrance. God, he was big. He was maybe a little bigger than Christian, whose thick cock had barely fit into her mouth. But Ryder was gentle as he'd promised, pressing against her slow and steady until the swollen head of his cock was entirely inside her.

And *fuck* that felt good. It felt good to be stretched and filled and taken like a woman, not like an obligation, and the rush of pleasure at their approval and frank desire was heady, sending pulses of heat and lust winding cords up her back. Her nipples pebbled into swollen points and her clit pulsed with need.

"More," she moaned, trying to thrust against Ryder's body to take more herself. But Christian distracted her with a dangerous game, fingers skirting the undersides of her breasts, which were now plump with desire. The second she lifted her hips off the picnic table, they would both hold her down and deny her any release.

"You want more, city girl?" Ryder asked, his pace oh so slow. "Ask me nicely." How did he have so much fucking control when she'd already come that night and still felt the world falling out from under her?

"Please?"

Christian swatted one of her swollen nipples and the pain made her skin sizzle and her breath catch.

"Don't they have manners in the city?" he queried, as though they were actually talking about San Fran and not his friend's cock buried deep in her pussy.

"*Tease*," she growled. Both men grinned. "Please fuck me, Ryder...*oh, God*. Fill my pussy with your big cock. I need... *I need...*"

Ryder thumbed small circles around her clit and made it impossible to breathe. Lights danced at the corners of her vision, her orgasm soaring higher.

"I need you to fill me up, come hard in my tight cunt...oh, *God*." She screamed it just as Ryder filled her all the way, slamming balls-deep into her body with an aching groan and she shot off somewhere, stars popping behind her eyelids, body bowing in a wild arc on the tabletop, her words tangled in a string of curses and prayers.

Finally, slowly, she came back to herself. Ryder's wicked, smug grin was only matched by Christian's dark, intense gaze.

"Again," Christian growled. "Come again." He looked down the table. "How does she feel, Ry? Is she tight around your cock? Milking you hard when she comes?"

God, those words were *filthy* and her whole body buzzed back to life in an instant. What? She *was* going to come again and soon? *Huh.*

"So *tight*," Ryder said through gritted teeth. His cock surged and throbbed inside her and Madison took comfort in not being the only one whose world had burst then been put back together.

She pushed the thought away and slid her hand around Christian's erection. The soft skin melded against her hand and he rocked hard into her touch. Then Ryder was moving in earnest too, riding her rough and fast, and she stroked Christian's cock with the same desperate rhythm. Ryder filled her and pulled almost all the way out before sliding hot and deep back into her. He seemed to get bigger every time he entered her body, filling her, making her arch and ache and groan.

And, despite her having just come, another release rose deep in her belly. She stroked Christian's cock even faster, bucking up to meet Ryder's thrusts and reveling in the deep groans torn from the back of his throat.

"So close, baby," Ryder growled, "I wanna feel you coming around my cock when I finish—will you do that for me?"

Madison didn't have a choice. She looked up at Christian, her mind fueled by lust and heat.

"Come in my mouth while Ryder's fucking me," she demanded, loving the heated expression that crossed the dark brown eyes. "Fuck my mouth, *please*." She damn near moaned the last and Christian slid his leaking cock across her lips. He pulled back, slapped his cock lightly against one of her cheeks and Madison moaned, her whole body shuddering.

"Like that, do ya?" Christian asked. He pulled back and slapped her a little harder, the sound fleshy and carnal. Her reaction was unexpected, but Madison couldn't deny each surge of wet heat that flooded her body when Christian cock-slapped her.

"One more, baby. I'll slap you one more time," he said on a moan. He slapped rough, really rough, smacking the side of her face hard with his thick erection and not stopping before he slid it between her lips. "So fucking sexy, swallowing my cock. Take it deep, you fucking angel." Christian's groans were almost indiscernible, but each dangerous, laden word was hot as fucking fire.

Then she was there, right *there*, and Ryder pumped once, twice, three times, just as Christian tweaked one of her swollen nipples and she lost it, bucking and groaning and spilling her juices all over Ryder's cock. It must have set him off, because he thrust twice more before settling his balls deep against her ass and shooting thick, hot cum into the condom deep inside her, his cock pumping.

A moment later, Christian jerked his hips and slid his cock down her throat, pumping his own sticky strands of cum with a deep, heady groan. He rested for a breath then stepped back from her mouth. Ryder pulled out carefully and slid the condom off to toss it in the trash.

Madison just stared up at the brilliant blue sky of the June night. Triple Diamond was gorgeous and she had just enjoyed the best sex of her whole damned life. *Ha, it's damn near enough to make a woman want to stay.*

Chapter Six

"Come on, city girl," Ryder said, picking his wet pants up off the ground. "Let's get you cleaned up."

Madison went to stand, but Christian didn't give her the chance. Instead, he picked her up off the picnic table as if she didn't weigh a damn thing. Oh, hell, she could *so* get used to this. Especially since he made it seem so damn easy to carry her into the house and up the stairs, his muscles seeming to not even strain under her weight. In the light of their house, Madison noticed something she hadn't seen before.

"You have a nipple ring?" She slid her finger over the cool silver piercing threaded through his left nipple.

"Yeah." Christian's voice was rough, husky with sex. "Do you like it?"

She didn't answer with words but instead wrapped her lips around the thin ring and sucked. Christian hissed and almost lost his footing. Behind them, Ryder chuckled. "He's a sensitive son of a bitch when you do that."

Hmm, I like the sound of that. "Think I could make you come just by sucking you here?" she asked, bold, sensual confidence inhabiting her mind and body like it never had before.

"If you give me about ten minutes, I say you're welcome to try," Christian replied, lust already lacing his voice. God, the man was positively sex on a stick.

He carried her into what she guessed was one of several master suites and through another door into the bathroom. The room was masculine, furnished in dark woods and earth tones, but the giant hot tub bath caught her eye.

"So obvious," she said, laughing as Christian set her down on her feet. "My uncle must have paid you guys really well."

The men grinned and Ryder shrugged before speaking. "We built the house," he said with a shrug. Madison had to pick her mouth up off the ground. The image of these two hotties building their own house made her brain go haywire. College degrees, great at sex and they'd built a freakin' house. *Is there anything they can't do?*

"Damn," she murmured. "That's sexy as hell."

Ryder pressed against her back, running his hands up her goosebumping skin, and Christian came around to stand in front of her. Madison's word of the day was definitely *sandwich*.

"What's sexy as hell is the thought of you, dripping and soapy," Ryder murmured in her ear, pressing heated kisses to the back of her neck. "We need to warm you up. I did say that lake was cold." Right then, Madison wasn't cold.

Ryder bent down and turned the water on, pouring a healthy dose of soap into the tub as it filled up. It was big, but so were the guys, and sharing would be a tight fit—not that she minded all that much right now.

Christian worked the zipper of her dress, his fingers deft. The sundress, which she had spent too much money on to be wearing into a lake, stuck to her skin and the idea of fresh, clean water was right then very appealing—as was the company. Christian pushed the dress down, pausing to kiss the skin he revealed. Ryder wrapped his hands around her waist and pulled her flush against his body. God, she'd just come like crazy and already these men had her aching and grinding, desperate for more contact.

"Bath's ready," Ryder said, his voice husky, and a heady thrill raced through her from knowing she'd been the one to make a man like Ryder—sexy, self-possessed, one hundred percent confident—sound like *that*.

"We have to get you out of these clothes," Christian murmured against her ear, none too subtly dragging the length of his cock along her hip. Fuck, but she liked that, liked knowing how much she turned both of them on, liked the thick rush of power. She stepped away from him and shimmied the rest of the way out of the dress, letting it fall to the floor. She hadn't worn a bra and her panties were long gone, so she stood before them, bared for the first time and feeling hot under their gazes.

"I could get used to a sight like that," Ryder growled.

I could get used to the sound of your voice when I make you all hot and bothered. "Gentlemen." Madison sought *some* control when the whole world seemed to be spiraling out from under her feet. "I'm going to climb into that tub, then I'm going to watch you finish undressing, slowly, before you join me."

She liked telling them what to do, more so since it was clear that neither man had expected her to take charge like that. Just to make it a little sweeter, she bent over the rim of the tub to test the water, ass high in the air for their perusal, to make a slow, teasing climb into the bath.

"You're gonna kill me, city girl," Ryder groaned.

"Yeah, but what a way to go." Christian's laugh was tinged with husky want. "Did you have any more demands for us?"

Oh, she had demands, and more than could be met in a single night. For a fleeting second, Madison considered what it'd be like to stay at Triple Diamond, tempted and teased by these men every day, finding new and creative ways to coax pleasures and desires from one another. As quickly as the thought had come, she pushed it away. San Francisco was home. This was a detour — an unexpected and sexy detour.

"Not for right now," she said with a smirk, "but I'll be sure to tell you when I do. Now, if you don't mind, jeans off, please."

She'd always enjoyed watching men undress. With Joshua, back when they were even still having sex, it had been all about the grand finale, getting to climax as fast as possible. But there was something to be said about the slow burn, the build-up and temptation — and she had a whole hell of a lot of temptation shucking their pants right in front of her. Two pairs of jeans landed in wet heaps on the floor and Ryder and Christian both stood unabashed, naked and powerful, their bodies works of sleek, muscled art.

"Now, who's going to help me soap up?" she asked. She enjoyed how they moved to the tub, to her, lazy, confident wild jungle cats stalking their prey. *Very willing prey.*

"Be careful what you wish for, sugar," Ryder said. "We're the professionals when it comes to getting you wet..."

She laughed, but the joke sent zings of heat racing down her spine all over again. Was this what it was supposed to be like, wanting a lover so much her brain shut down and all she could think about was touching them, tasting them, having them over and over again? It was good the arrangement was temporary or she'd never get a single thing done.

Christian and Ryder climbed into the bath, and before she could protest — not that she had any plans for that — Christian pulled her into his lap, positioning her body so she couldn't deny what was on his mind.

Ryder slid in front of her, soaping up a washcloth and sliding it across her breasts in slow, maddening movements.

"You're so fucking gorgeous," Ryder said. His words were almost a growl. He bent and sucked one nipple into his mouth before pulling back. "Christian, her breasts are amazing."

Christian nipped the nape of her neck, sliding his tongue in a teasing trail across her skin.

"So is her ass," he murmured, "Feels so good, grinding against me."

Maybe there was something wrong with her. Good girls weren't supposed to get aroused by being talked about like a sex doll, as if she wasn't even in the same room as them. Or maybe the filthy conversation was just so sexy, so hot and arousing to hear that Madison couldn't resist. Either way, she didn't really give a damn, not with Christian's cock surging against the curve of her ass and Ryder's tempting fingers circling her swollen nipples.

"Are your breasts sensitive, Maddy?" Ryder asked without slowing his caresses. "Do you think I can make you come without touching anything else?"

They'd been playing her body like a damn violin. Taking her to climax was *when* not an *if*.

"You can try," she said, instead of the truth. *Never let them know how much power they have.* Not that she denied the flush across her skin or her shallow breathing — dead giveaways of her arousal.

Ryder flicked one nipple. "So much mouth," he said with a dangerous grin. "I think we should teach you some manners."

Heat rushed through her body when she imagined Ryder bending her over his lap and spanking her ass red. She squirmed.

"Oh, you like that, don't you?" Christian murmured low into her ear. "You're rubbing against my cock like a cat in heat. Do you want to be punished? Tied up and spanked? Tell us, city girl."

Her cheeks flamed, but, in truth, the window of opportunity for being embarrassed had closed a long time ago.

"I want to be spanked," she moaned on a breath. She pressed back against Christian while she spoke, still enjoying Ryder's fingers against her swollen breasts. *Oh, God, what if they make me come this way? I might not survive.*

"Where, baby?" Ryder whispered against her mouth. He dove into another possessive kiss and continued, "Where do you wanna to be spanked?"

His tone was so aroused that Madison gave in and spilled the fantasies that even her closest girlfriends didn't know anything about.

"My ass," she murmured, "and...and my nipples and..."

"And what?" Christian asked, gripping her ass below the water, his rough squeeze indicative of just how hot and bothered he was. Well, damn it, she was only acting like a cat in springtime because of their naughty promises.

"And my pussy," she whispered. "I want you to spank my pussy."

Christian's cock throbbed hard and she knew that both of them had slipped into the erotic fantasy alongside her.

"That's so hot, sugar," Ryder whispered. "Anytime you want to make that happen, you just misbehave and we'll punish you good."

Madison bowed against Christian, pressing her front into Ryder's. "I want..."

Ryder plucked a nipple, his fingers rough. "What do you want?" he asked. "You have to tell us."

She moaned, low and deep. "You," she murmured, "I want both of you." She'd only just had them and yet her body demanded more.

"So needy," Christian said. "But if you insist."

They lifted her free of the tub, two sets of hands toweling her dry in the cool bathroom, until her blood ran hot all over again. No more teasing, no more tempting. She wanted them right *now*.

Without waiting for either man, Madison walked into the adjoining bedroom and climbed onto the bed, resting against the headboard with anticipation and heat drumming through her entire body. In the doorway, Ryder and Christian both stood, large and imposing, sex and desire etched across their eyes. She was just a few short minutes away from a complete and utter explosion.

"What are you waiting for?" she challenged.

That did it. Ryder was on the bed in a second, Christian just behind him. Somehow, the men had communicated between themselves, their roles reversed from what they had been outside. Christian pulled her to the end of the bed and spread her legs wide. At the top of the bed, Ryder kissed her, challenging, promising.

She was wired so tightly, so ready to burst that when Christian slipped one thick finger between her folds, Madison nearly came on the spot.

"So wet," Christian murmured, sliding his finger free and tasting it in a deliberate and hot-as-fuck display. "I can't wait to feel how tight you are around my cock."

He stepped away for a moment and moved to the side table at the edge of the bed, pulled out a condom and sheathed his cock in one quick movement. Then he was back at her entrance, teasing and tempting. So close, but not close enough.

"Damn it," Madison moaned, "give it to me, now…please?" She arched her hips, desperate to take more of his cock.

"Better do what she says," Ryder murmured.

Despite the overwhelming onslaught of pleasure and desire taking over her body, Madison managed to look up at him. "Come here," she whispered, pulling him close, so his cock bobbed just in front of her mouth. She wetted her lips and parted them in invitation. Ryder slid his thick cock inside at the same moment Christian pressed into her body, parting her folds and filling her, deep and hard.

"So fucking tight," he growled, trying to leash his lust. "*Jesus*, you feel so good."

Madison moaned around Ryder's cock and he slid his hand into her hair, holding tight.

"Think you can ride us both, sugar?" he asked. "Take Christian's cock in your tight little hole while I fuck your mouth? That's what you want, isn't it?"

She moaned around his cock again, relaxing her throat so she could take him to the back. A thin line of spit escaped, sliding down Ryder's thick shaft.

"Fucking love you drooling on my cock," he growled. "I could watch you choke on it all day."

Her pussy clenched at the filthy words and Christian let out a rough curse.

"Keep talking to her like that," he growled. "She fucking likes being told what to do, don't you, baby?"

It was a rhetorical question, but she bucked in response, taking his cock even deeper, until his balls pressed against her legs. She felt full and stretched and so fucking hot she was about to explode.

Then they moved in unison, taking and filling and giving her exactly what she wanted — what she needed — until Madison's vision swam and her coming release tingled at the base of her spine. She thrust forward and back to meet both of their movements, taking and giving in equal measure until her motions became jerky and uncoordinated, elation coursing through her aching body.

"Just give in, Maddy," Christian whispered, and Ryder pushed her hair out of her eyes. "We'll be here to catch you."

The small tenderness did it, among everything else, and Madison bowed forward once, twice, once more before pleasure overtook her and crowded her mind and everything else in the room disappeared. The men sped up their movements, until Ryder pumped hot and hard into her mouth, following the tails of her orgasm. Below her, Christian thrust again, just once more, then he, too, came

They all collapsed onto the bed. Madison's heart was pounding a thousand miles a minute and she tried to steady her breathing. She hadn't come that many times in her entire relationship with Joshua, let alone in one insane, depraved night. But that was *all* this was, just one night — or a few nights or whatever — to air out her frustrations, before she sold the ranch and returned to San Francisco. Which was just what she wanted. *Of course, it is.*

"If you're still thinking that much, we didn't do our job properly," Ryder said. He propped himself up on one elbow to look at her. "What's going through that mind of yours?"

She smiled, a sleepy, contented smile, the kind of smile she hadn't used in months. This was just a fun affair, nothing more — nothing to get worked up over.

"Nothing at all," she said, sliding up the bed until she rested against the plush pillows. "I'm just sleepy. You guys tired me out."

The men exchanged looks then both got up to leave. Madison shook her head, the action quick and tight.

"Stay with me," she said, her eyes already drooping closed. "Please?"

Because she missed having someone beside her in bed — because she needed a reminder that this was real, *she* was still real, after all the unreal stuff that had happened this week.

Christian and Ryder both nodded and climbed into the large bed, snuggling up on either side of her. As Madison fell asleep, contented, satisfied, she couldn't ignore the distant, passing thought of just how easy it would be to get used to a life like this.

Chapter Seven

She might be the most beautiful woman he had ever seen. Scratch that, she was for sure the most beautiful woman he'd ever seen. The early morning sun cut lazy streaks across the bed, catching golden strands of her rich, chestnut hair, and Christian contented himself with watching her soft breathing, the rise and fall of her bare chest. Her skin was pale, nothing a few days out in the summer sun couldn't tan golden, but so soft to the touch that it was hard to resist putting his lips to her shoulders, breasts and soft, supple thighs that had brought such pleasure.

For a second, guilt clenched at his belly. He and Ryder had decided that keeping her in the dark was the best way to wrangle up the money to buy their share of the ranch before she got the chance to sell it outright. Not telling her the truth had seemed like a good idea last night, before they'd gotten to talking to her, about the big things and the small, before they'd had her over and over, all night long. Maddy—Madison—Hollis was passionate, and a deep part of him ached to know her better, to understand each quirk, what made her tick, how to make that brilliant, dazzling smile spread across her cheeks.

Not that this was ever intended to be anything more than what it was — a summer fling. He and Ryder had indulged in more than their fair share of those. But, despite having known her for only two days, Christian couldn't deny that there was something altogether different about her from any other woman he'd ever been with. Gone was the desire to push her buttons, unless they were the kind of buttons that made her scream. Gone was the need to make her want to leave. In their places was a whole tangle of emotions that very much involved getting her to stay — right there where she was in this bed, pressing against him.

"Christian." She whispered his name in a soft, breathy moan and all the blood in his body ran straight from his brain to his cock. Her eyes were still closed and she was still facing slightly away from him, but her fingers moved, beckoning him closer. Well, damn, he wasn't about to resist a demand from a lush, naked woman in bed. "Come here."

He fit their naked bodies together and pressed his erection against her full ass, sending erotic trills down his spine, and fought not to slam up against her. Jesus *fuck,* this woman got him hard doing nothing more than whispering his name.

"Where's Ryder?" she asked, eyes still closed, voice laden with sleep.

For once, Christian was grateful for Ryder's absence, enjoying Maddy's touch, her soft skin for his own. Normally, he got off on the erotic nature of sharing a woman with his best friend, but right now he wanted her all to himself.

"Running some errands," Christian murmured, that familiar guilt seizing him again. Wolf Creek was a farming town, which meant a lot of the businesses got their work down before folks had to tend to the animals and crops. It wasn't even quarter after five, but Ryder had driven into town to visit the community bank before work started for the day, hoping to get answers about their shares of Triple Diamond — answers Christian wasn't so sure he wanted anymore.

But he distracted himself and kissed the back of her neck. Maddy squirmed a little and paused when she felt his growing erection nestled between her ass cheeks. She laughed, soft and breathy.

"Is that your normal morning wood?" she asked, "because *hello*, cowboy." Her still sleepy tone added a whole dose of *Jesus fucking cute* to the sexy-as-hell words.

"That's all you, Maddy," Christian murmured against her neck. God, he just wanted to touch all of her. "Do you want me to see when Ryder's getting home?" Not that Christian felt any inclination to talk about Ryder when he was a breath away from sinking his cock deep into her heat. But instead of answering, Maddy wiggled against him and his cock surged. Christian put his hand on her hips and steadied her movements with a growl.

"Be careful what you ask for you, city girl," he said. "You're making me crazy, pressing this plush ass against my cock." For emphasis, and because he couldn't seem to stop himself, Christian pinched one round cheek.

"I know *exactly* what I'm asking for," Maddy said, all traces of sleep gone from her voice. "And if you don't get a condom on in the next ten seconds, I'll start without you."

Christian moved as she spoke, tearing open the bedside table drawer and grabbing a condom as fast as he could.

"As much as I'd enjoy watching you fuck yourself," he said, because *damn*, that image did things to his brain he wasn't sure were legal, "I'm much prefer to be buried deep inside your sweet pussy myself." He put on the condom in one quick motion and lined up behind her.

"What do you want, Maddy?" he asked, as if the soft mewls of desire and want weren't spilling unchecked from her lips.

"Tease," she moaned. "Give it to me."

He would have liked to tempt her more, he really would have. But already Christian's blood was boiling and his desire ratcheting up to eleven. This woman turned him *volcanic*.

He spread her legs wide and sank deep into her waiting pussy. God, she was tight. In this position, with her legs wrapped around him, it wouldn't be long until he lost control and gave her everything. And part of him really wanted to give her everything.

"Christian." When she moaned his name, his cock throbbed deep inside her. "Oh, God, please move."

Well, how can I resist a request like that? He slid nearly all the way out of her body before pressing back into her, creating a push and pull of movement, and within seconds she accepted the pace. She met him thrust for thrust, each touch another zing of electricity that burned up his spine and made him ache for release. But it just felt so fucking good and he wanted it to last, wanted to stay buried in her heat as long as he fucking could.

"I'm so close," she moaned, face half-buried in the sheets. "Come with me, Christian, please?"

Christian pounded faster and harder, bringing his fingers around to stroke her clit as he filled her and stretched her…

"*There…*" Maddy's voice broke on a scream and she came in a tight, pulsing heat that clenched his cock. The sensation sent Christian right over the edge, too, and with one more thrust of his hips, he pulsed long and hot into the condom, filling her tight body.

For a moment, they lay there, catching their breath until finally, slowly, he slid free of her body and moved to clean up. He ran a washcloth under the water then returned to the bedroom. He could definitely get used to the sight of Maddy spread out and boneless. She stretched her hand out for the washcloth, but Christian shook his head. Instead, he cleaned her body himself, using soft, slow strokes, until she was shimmery and oh so soft.

Something inside him grew a little tight at the idea, but he shook it off.

"That is one hell of a way to wake up," she murmured, half into the pillow. Her voice ran husky with spent desire and his cock twitched in interest. Something about this woman, about making her come, about holding her through the night, made him positively carnal.

"It's my favorite way," Christian said. "Did you get enough sleep? We went to bed pretty late last night."

She rolled on her side and looked up at him, a sardonic expression crossing her hooded, sleepy gaze.

"And whose fault was that?" she asked.

Just because he could, Christian reached out and plucked her nipple. She gasped and shivered and he cocked his head to the side.

"Yours, as far as I recall. Something about *needing us, wanting us, now, now, now…*"

She pursed her lips but couldn't keep the smile off her face.

"I'll concede to being the one who kept you up, but I definitely didn't say any of that." The teasing expression in her eyes told Christian she knew for a fact that she had. "And I'm more than rested — with my nutty schedule, I'm lucky to get five and a half hours a night."

Christian frowned. He wasn't unaccustomed to a heavy workload — that was life on a farm, up with the sun and no weekends off. But he didn't like the way her voice sounded, and even though he didn't need that much sleep to function, five and a half hours a night just wasn't enough after a while.

"Do you need to work that hard?" he asked. "I mean, they're what, parties and conferences? Not the end of the world."

She laughed, but he didn't like the sound, a little tired and a whole lot of self-effacing.

"You're being awfully nice to me, Mr. Badass." He scowled, which only made her laugh again. "But if you want the truth, no, I didn't want to do corporate events. When I graduated UCLA and Daniels and Hark offered me the position, I couldn't turn it down. It pays really well and the work is challenging and interesting, but…I don't know. I feel like something might be missing."

He stroked her hair, a little disturbed with how content he felt just lying here beside her in the early morning sun. He *was* being really nice to her, far nicer than was smart. And he couldn't have stopped himself if the sky had started falling.

"Well, if you didn't want to do corporate," he asked, "what did you want to do?"

At that, her smile brightened, all remnants of that niggling frustration leaving her face.

"Weddings, actually," she said. "They don't pay as well and I'd have to start my own business if I wanted to make enough to continue living in San Francisco, since it's just so freaking expensive, but I always saw myself doing weddings. I don't know. I have time..." she trailed off. "Why agricultural engineering?"

Christian didn't miss the change of subject, but he let it go. It was evident that she had to work through her own career issues before he got involved. Not that he had *any* plans to get involved.

"I guess I just had a head for numbers." He shrugged. "Mason gave us jobs here when we were fourteen, and not long after, I started suggesting changes to him. He always gave me a chance—some were miserable failures, but others turned out really well. When he offered to send us to college, I realized that I really loved making the ranch function to the best of its ability, so I focused on how to do that."

She stroked his face, sending a shiver down Christian's back. "You are full of surprises, Christian Harlow," she said. "All tough guy on the outside, but there's so much more to you than that."

The breath caught in Christian's chest and he froze like a stone. How long had people seen him as the inked-up troublemaker, despite his degree and expertise? And here she was, not two days in his life, and she'd breached the dark surface to *see* him, even though *him* had been a real asshole to her from the start.

"I hear Ryder's truck," he said, all of a sudden needing space to breathe. "Want breakfast?"

She rose from the bed, giving him a bright smile while she dressed, as though unfazed by the abruptness of his departure.

"No one's cooked me breakfast in a long time," she said. "Can you make pancakes?"

Christian laughed. "I can make one hell of a pancake."

Chapter Eight

Ryder walked into the kitchen, surprised to be greeted by so many delicious scents. He raised an eyebrow at Christian, who appeared to be...cooking? Hmm. *This is confusing, if not just that little bit alarming.*

"Hey, I can cook," Christian said, shooting him a dark look. Either he'd spoken aloud, or Christian was just way too good at reading him. "I just let you think I can't so you'll feed me."

Ryder was damn sure that Christian's sudden desire to make — *Jesus Christ, are those chocolate chip pancakes?* — had nothing to do with him and everything to do with the slight, beautiful woman wearing one of Christian's Harley tank tops and nothing else, sitting propped up on the kitchen counter. Damn, she really didn't look like a city girl now, not with the softness in her lips and eyes, or the messy way her hair curled down her back and across her shoulders. If they managed to coax *this* out of her in just a day, he could only imagine what they could do with a week or more.

Guilt clenched in Ryder's belly. He'd spent the last half an hour at the bank, going over Mason's will and the requirements for a loan. All *should* have been good news. The law was on their side when it came to purchasing the land and their collateral for those last few thousand bucks checked out.

But if it was good news, then why did it make Ryder feel like he'd drunk too much moonshine? Maybe they should just tell her the truth about the whole thing. The formidable, intimidating woman who had stepped out of the white BMW in high heels just one day ago was nowhere in sight. Instead, sitting on his damn kitchen counter, the smiling, half-naked goddess who had fucked both their brains out the night before was at that moment sucking chocolate off Christian's finger while he laughed.

And that sight made Ryder feel a little odd. Not guilty but…jealous? No, they'd shared plenty of lovers in the past, and never once had ego or envy gotten in the way of a good time. And that was all this was — a good time, a way to keep Maddy Hollis *distracted* while they cobbled together the money to buy her family ranch out from under her nose. Put that way, the decision to keep her in the dark made Ryder feel like shit at the bottom of his boots after a day in the barn. And he sure as hell couldn't be thinking of her as Maddy, even if the fool nickname had stuck in his mind the very first time Christian had used it. Maddy was so much softer than Madison. It was *this* version of her, compared to the one from when she'd first arrived.

He didn't deserve her softness. Her freckles and her laugh and her long, tempting legs made him ache, and not just physically. Part of him wished he were the one making her breakfast, feeding her chocolate chips and making her smile. But Ryder had long ago come to grips with the truth — some people weren't destined for love and he was one of them. Dear old Dad had made damn sure he knew it, and still, some days, he wondered why Christian's dad, Bill, and Mason had bothered to take him in, even after all they knew about where he'd grown up. It had been some fifteen years since he'd left his dad's house — shack — and still the wounds simmered below the surface of his memories, disturbed by too much movement or thinking in the direction of the past.

He must have had quite the scowl on his face, because when Ryder glanced back over to Christian and *Madison*, they were both staring at him with confused expressions. Hers was sweeter, more innocent and questioning, but Christian's look said six ways to Sunday he knew just what was going on in Ryder's brain. About Madison, maybe, and more than maybe about his dad, too. *And fuck all to that.* Ever since he'd moved in with Christian, escaping his own tragic family history to finish high school, his best friend had been able to read him like a fucking open book. For once, in a damn long time, Ryder didn't want Christian in his head.

"I'm going to the barn," he said, his voice gruffer than he meant it to be, as shown by Christian raising his eyebrow and a shadow of sadness passing across Madison's pretty dark eyes. His heart softened, just a little. She was just so *pretty*. A smattering of freckles danced across the bridge of her nose, ones that hadn't been there yesterday. He liked half-naked, no-makeup Maddy a lot more than the city-girl version.

"I'm being grumpy," he said, and placed a soft kiss on her cheek.

She looked up at him and smiled. "Duty calls."

He nodded. "Everyone's about to have a baby these days. I have to do my maternity rounds." Then, because he couldn't stop himself, Ryder leaned down and kissed Maddy's swollen pink lips in a rough embrace. She tasted like chocolate and sunshine and something summery and free and completely addicting. "Thanks for the pancake." He snatched one off the plate and took a big bite, winking at Maddy when Christian squawked. "You know where to find me," Ryder tossed over his shoulder.

Usually, the barn offered him solace, an escape from the sometimes-oppressive memories of his childhood and, more recently, the grief that threatened to overwhelm him with Mason's passing. The place's comforting earthy scents and animal chatter was his escape, a reminder that he had a shiny degree and a *doctor* in front of his name and achievements and successes, all the ones everyone had always said a Dean boy could never get. Well, he'd worked hard for them and now he lived his dream, spending the day with animals, caring and tending for them. Animals had always been less complicated than people.

But even the horses and goats didn't offer their normal respite from his churning thoughts. When the barn door opened and shut a little while later, he almost jumped out of his skin at the sound.

"I didn't mean to spook you," Maddy said. She wore a pair of dark jeans that looked mighty expensive for where she stood in a barn full of pregnant horses, and a flowing white tank top that made him ache to taste her again, to touch her and explore her body they way they'd passed the night.

"Not spooked," he said, though they both knew he was lying. Less than a full day after arriving, this woman made him nervous and excited in the schoolboy way that set him on edge, a way he hadn't acted since asking Kitty Scranton to prom.

"You seemed upset this morning," she said, not pointing out the obvious lie. Instead of continuing, however, she walked around the edge of the barn, communicating with each animal she passed and, despite the expensive clothes, despite his own first impression, she looked as though she belonged there, among the animals. In his barn. With him.

Back off, Ryder.

"I'm sorry I was an ass," he said, wiping horseshoe grease off his hands before walking over to her. She looked up at him with hesitation in her face, as if she wasn't certain where they stood. Ryder hated that she felt unsure around him, though he was no closer to naming this thing between them than she was.

"I was worried," Maddy admitted, her low voice taking him by surprise. She raised her hand, cupping his cheek in a way both familiar and innocent. The simple touch just about undid him. He didn't just want her—he *ached* for her with a fierceness that took his breath and made every thought in his mind go blank. "What's in this head of yours, Ryder Dean?" she murmured. "Inquiring minds want to know."

He shifted his face in her hand, just enough to kiss the soft flesh of her palm. All the air had gone out of the barn and Ryder was in free fall.

"Inquiring minds will be sorry they asked," he said. "There's a whole lot in there even I don't want to think about."

She shook her head. "I'm just starting to understand why we have to talk about those things most of all." Glancing up at the horse before her, Dolly, Maddy continued, "Do you mind talking about Mason?"

Though his name made Ryder's heart hurt a little, he shook his head. "It'd be my pleasure to talk about Mason. What do you want to know?"

Maddy sighed and grew visibly frustrated. "I don't even know. I lost my parents when I was a kid. Grew up with my dad's brother's family. I don't know much of anything about my mom's family at all."

There was so much grief and tragedy rolled into a few simple sentences that Ryder simply pulled Madison close and held her. She took a few shallow breaths against his chest and, when she looked up at him, her eyes were glassy.

"Mason was a good man," he said, his voice a little gravelly and husky. "Anyone would have been lucky to call him family. I certainly felt that way and I know Christian did, too. Christian, his dad Bill, and Mason are the men I respect most in this world."

He didn't miss her questioning gaze and, while he might have ignored it for another person, something about this woman made Ryder open his mouth and give the answer to her unasked question.

"My daddy was a real sick son of a bitch," he admitted, still hating to say it after all these years. "Took the bottle like a duck to water. My momma passed when I was still a kid, then he took to beating me the way he used to beat on her. I finally got strong enough to see past it when I got a little older and Bill took me in and I lived with them from when I was sixteen to when I left for college." And though those memories had been with him for over a decade, it still felt raw and intimate to tell another person, hell, a stranger, even if she didn't exactly feel like one. Desperate to get away from the past, he asked "What about you? Grow up with your cousins?"

Maddy nodded, her eyes sad. "One cousin, Lily. She's my Christian." She said the last sentence with the painful twist of a smile. "Best friend in the whole world. She runs a flower shop in San Francisco, down the street from my office."

Her self-effacing tone made Ryder raise an eyebrow. "So close and worlds apart?" he asked, seeing something just below the surface.

She laughed, but there was no spark of humor in those rich brown eyes. "You could say that. I don't know. I guess I get jealous of her or something. She works night and day to keep the place alive, but, damn, she's so happy. Lils followed her dream, you know? She's the boss of her own life. That all seems really nice sometimes."

Ryder tipped Maddy's chin up so he could look her in the eye. "Why not leave?" The second his words hit the air, something glowed in his chest, something he had no right to feel. To *hope*. "Why stay with your job if you feel that way?"

She knit her brows and pursed her lips in an approximation of a rueful grin. "Well, up until a week ago, I didn't exactly have anything else doing. Though, I suppose with the ranch profits, I could do just about anything I wanted." A different sensation clanged in his chest that time, the sound as heavy and echoing as a metal pipe falling down a well. He needed to tell her the truth, about their deal with Mason, about how they had kind of sort of used her, seduced her into distraction. Okay, so that hadn't been a hardship.

They'd have done it, anyway, since neither of them seemed able to keep their eyes or hands off her, but something was changing here and she damn well deserved the truth.

But he needed to talk to Christian first. They'd gone into this stupid-ass plan together, but it wasn't just that. Deep down, they were brothers and Christian deserved as much a say in the matter as Ryder did, or at least a heads-up regarding what Ryder was going to do.

"What would you want to do?" he asked, "if you could do anything?"

She paused to think about that for a moment before slowly replying, "Well, I've always loved events, but I think I'd liked to be more in charge, run my own business or something, instead of having to answer to my bosses. I told Christian this morning, I'd always wanted to do weddings, no more of this corporate shit. It just gets so old and dull. When I'm planning a really great event, I get inspired, ya know? It's been a long time since I've been inspired."

If he were smart, and he considered himself smart, with the whole Dr. in front of his name thing, then he'd hightail it on the next train out of Montana. Because watching this strong, powerful woman struggle with a sense of self, confident despite her lack of direction, so brutally honest with him in the wake of their short-lived connection, it made him want things — and not just physical things either. Though the expression of deep concentration on her face had him wanting that too, as did the intimacy of the room.

"Ryder?" Her voice was husky and sweet as tea and at that moment he had a sharp craving for the taste of chocolate chip pancakes on her lips. With the slowest of deliberation, he raised one eyebrow and she let out a soft laugh. "Don't look at me like that!"

Mmm, he liked her tone, laughing and aroused all at once. He loomed over her, stepping forward until he had her pressed against the barn wall.

"Like what, city girl?" he asked, his voice betraying the rising desire wreaking havoc on his control.

"Like you want to eat me," she whispered. *Wench.* She knew exactly how those words affected him. The image of her bent over, hands against the wall and long legs spread wide, crossed Ryder's mind and now it was the only thing he could see.

"Sugar, if you doubt how much I wanna eat you, I didn't do a very good job last night."

Her cheeks reddened, a contrast that was surprising in its innocence to the heat pooling behind those dark eyes.

"I don't quite remember," she said, her voice more moan than whisper. "Maybe you should remind me."

His own reply was nothing short of a growl. "It would be my pleasure." He brought his mouth to hers in a desperate tangle, raked his hand through her soft hair and pulled her as close to his body as possible. But it wasn't enough. With this demanding, passionate woman, he didn't know if it would ever be enough.

As they kissed, he quickly unbuttoned her jeans then unzipped them and pushed them down her legs. He reached out and grabbed a handful of her plump ass, squeezing hard. Maddy squealed and arched up into his body, pressing supple flesh against his rigid cock, and Ryder groaned before sinking to his knees in the hay.

He pressed soft, heated kisses to her lace-covered pussy, each stroke drawing another long, hot moan from Maddy's mouth, and it wasn't long before he licked, sucked and pressed his own desperate mouth to her panties. Fuck, it made him a little unhinged to bring her pleasure. He slid her jeans down further, just enough to get her scrap of panties out of the way, revealing her swollen, glistening pussy.

Ryder moved to take off his Stetson, but Maddy stayed his movements with a hand around his wrist.

"Leave the hat on."

Her demand sent fire straight to his cock and his balls tightened, hot and heavy, responding to the growl in her voice. If she wanted to fuck a cowboy, he was more than happy to volunteer for the position — any position.

"Yes, ma'am," he murmured, then tongued her opening, probing her hole. Maddy was responsive and so fucking sexy, with her breathy moans and the way she clutched at the air, signaling she was nearing her release. But Ryder didn't just want her to come — he wanted her to fucking explode all over his mouth, so he thumbed her clit, swirling it around in rough, jerky motions while he tongue-fucked her, until Maddy shook and moaned, breaking apart all over him, screaming his name like a prayer in a hurricane.

His cock surged in response to her shuddering, her body hot and tight and so sexy he might finish right then and there. Instead, he stood, caressing her still trembling body until her breathing slowed and her gaze came back into focus.

"I think you might have just killed me," she whispered on a laugh. "Jesus, that was incredible."

"Ryder will do just fine," he said, unable to stop his cocky grin from spreading. Maddy gave him an amused look, her face still satisfied and, oh, so delicious.

"Will he now?" she teased him with one raised eyebrow. She brought her hands around his waist. "Why don't you prove it?"

And with that, Ryder was on her, kissing her like a man possessed, her lips, her neck, the swelling curves of her breasts. He undid his jeans, yanked a condom out of his back pocket and pulled it on in what must have been record time. Fisting his cock in his hand, he groaned into her ear.

"Are you ready for me, sugar?" Her soft mewl in response was delicious and so fucking tempting.

"Please," she begged, with just enough innocence in her voice to make him want to pump deep inside her.

He nipped at her ear. "Please *what?*"

She didn't pretend not to understand. "Please *fuck* me," she groaned. "I want your cock. Now, Ryder, *please?*"

How can a man resist a request like that? Ryder lined his cock up to her pussy and pressed inside. Her walls clutched hot around him. God, she was so tight he felt crazed and heated and needy all at once.

"Gotta move, baby," he said. "Please." Now it was him begging, for release, for anything that might relieve some of the insane pressure mounting within him.

"Oh, God, move. Please move," Maddy begged, clenching her pussy and making Ryder's whole body burn. Which was when he did move, pulling out slowly then burying his cock deep, the thrusts growing harder and faster. He started losing control, giving over to the sheer carnality of fucking and filling and taking her hard and fast, over and over.

Maddy grasped at the wall behind her, eyes glazing over, breath coming in short, desperate pants, her breasts bouncing and pressing against him.

"More, more, *more.*" She broke on the last, coming apart against her evident pleasure and screaming his name. Her tight cunt squeezed his cock so hard that Ryder's control spiraled out from under him and he burst free, pumping and riding his release as he spilled jet after jet of hot cum into the condom, emptying his full balls into the sexiest woman he'd ever fucking met.

"You're so good at that." Her tone was a little husky and a lot rough, and he liked knowing he was the one who had made her sound like *that.*

"Team effort," he said, nipping at her neck. He tossed the condom into the trash and slid his zipper closed. "You make me crazy, Maddy. Totally unhinged."

She smiled a dangerous kind of smile. Then she pushed off the wall and walked toward the door. "Good," she said. Then she slipped out of sight.

Chapter Nine

"I don't know, Lils, life is so much slower out here. I have to say, it's kind of nice." Madison pressed the phone between her ear and shoulder, pulling clothes out of her suitcase as she caught her cousin up on everything that had happened over the past few days. Well, not *everything*. The men—not her men, just *the* men—would be coming back in from work pretty soon and she wanted to chat with Lily before she got distracted. Again.

"Well, obviously I don't want you to go anywhere," Lily said, the busy sounds of her downtown San Francisco flower shop coming over the line. "But if you do decide to ride this one for a while, I'm in full support. You work too hard, Mads. Daniels and Hark works you too hard. I keep telling you that."

Madison sighed, somehow not responding to the inadvertent *ride this one*. Was she cracked to consider staying there, even for the smallest amount of time? Hell, if the initial sales estimate was anywhere near correct in its valuation of Triple Diamond, she wouldn't need to work another day for three reincarnations, let alone eighty hours a week. It was *tempting,* even if she couldn't quite figure out if it was the ranch and open skies that was pulling her east of California, or something else entirely.

Maybe those two hot cowboys wormed their way into my mind more than I want to admit. No, that'd be crazy. She'd only arrived a few days ago but found herself thinking about them in spare moments between paperwork for the bank and remote work for her job. And more than just her spare moments, too. Fine, almost all her moments. Except it was just about sex—nothing else whatsoever—like the security she had taken in waking in Christian's arms, or the way Ryder had opened up to her in the barn, made her feel comfortable enough to open up to him.

Yeah, not thinking about any of that at all. Right.

"God damn it," Lillian said, her light and airy tone a stark contrast to the curse, and it snapped Madison back to reality.

"What's up, Lils?" she asked. She found a black teddy at the bottom of her bag and held it up in front of her body before the mirror, then she tossed it on the bed and dug around for the black pumps she knew were in there somewhere. Maybe after dinner she'd surprise Ryder and Christian with some of her sexier stuff. Lucy jumped up from her spot on the floor in the sun and settled right down in the middle of Madison's expensive French lingerie. *Furry little shit.*

"Just work," Lillian said. "I have a wildflower-themed wedding coming up and my order of *arnica Montana* flowers froze en route. It's super in this season and a real pain in the ass to get my hands on."

Madison twisted her lips. "Montana?" she asked. "What does it look like?" She peered out of the window at the vast expanse of farmland and mountain ranges. Christian had told her a little about the commercial agriculture but she didn't know anything about the wildflowers growing just past the edge of the Triple Diamond irrigation systems.

"It looks like a wild flower," Lillian grumbled. "Your basic yellow wildflower. It's pretty but I am *so* not a fan right now."

"Hmm, maybe I can convince the guys to grow you some," Madison considered out loud. The sudden silence on the phone was loud as hell and she swore she could *hear* Lily raise her eyebrow.

"The guys?" she asked, "Madison…"

"Nothing," Madison cut in, far too quickly to alleviate any curiosity—Lils was a shark when it came to these things. Better to quit while she was ahead. "It's nothing. But think about it. I'll run away from my big city job and become your wholesale flower exporter. It'll be a family business!" She didn't tack on the *having the world's hottest sex with the world's hottest cowboys every night* addendum. That, she was saving for herself.

"It does sound nice," Lillian replied. "Maybe don't be so quick to write off making a change. And I'm not just saying that because I'd love to have you as my wholesaler."

Madison had meant it as a joke. She really had. But the idea—the fantasy—was a little sticky now, like it wasn't quite letting go. Her mind swam with planning. Just for fun. Finding bakeries for the cakes, decorators and tent supplies, florists, musicians and caterers…

"I won't write it off completely," she said, feeling a little odd in the face of her excitement at the prospect.

There was a knock at the door and Madison looked up, before adding, "But I have to go, work to do and all. I'll call you if I find the flowers you need, all right?"

"Sounds good," Lillian said, her tone far too knowing for Madison's liking. Could she tell over the phone that Madison was contemplating the massive upheaval of her life? More like Madison was just being paranoid, given just how insane the whole idea of it was. "I love you, Mads. Whatever choice you make, I'll support you."

"Love you, too, Lils," Madison replied, also reverting back to their childhood nicknames before they both clicked off. The last time she'd had a nickname, she and Lillian had been kids. Until now. Until this weekend and her two hunka-hunka cowboys who had been occupying her every thought.

Mmm, I'm getting used to being called Maddy.

Shut up, Madison.

It was a little scary and a little exciting all at once. Because she liked the independence the Triple Diamond Ranch provided, liked knowing she was now the one in charge of the decision to stay or leave her job. Hell, how much would she miss San Fran, in truth? Lily and her parents, who had adopted her after the car crash, were all still in Cali. But Madison didn't love her job and didn't have any sort of social life because of it and since things with Joshua had all gone so tits up…
Hmm, maybe sticking around is something worth considering.

Another knock sounded and she called out. Ryder opened the door, a sexy, lazy smile on his face, and it made Madison feel calmer, somehow, safe and comforted. Maybe she'd bring up staying with him and

Christian, just to see what they thought of the idea. For some reason, it really mattered what they thought.

"What's up?" she asked, trying to shake the cobwebs of confusion and doubt from her mind. His grin only widened.

"Get your stuff, sugar. We're going camping."

Madison blinked into the doorway, where Ryder stood with a small bag slung over one shoulder and a devilish grin on his face. He knew just what she thought about camping and there wasn't a doubt in her mind that he was enjoying teasing her.

"What?" The word held all of her incredulity and distaste, and Madison tossed her phone on the bed. Lily would have laughed her ass off at the idea of all-grown-up Madison camping. Maybe she *should* go, just to prove she could.

"You heard me," Ryder said. God, he was just so big and she felt so tiny in comparison to his broad chest and the obvious strength of his shoulders and arms. Camping. With him. *Dangerous territory.*

"I don't want to go camping…" Her tone signaled a question, but it came out more as *you know I don't want to go camping, so why are you asking me?*

"I know you don't." He stepped into the room, which had felt large and spacious until he'd arrived. Now she felt like she couldn't breathe, squeezed into the space with a hot cowboy who made her want to lick *everywhere.* "But there are two reasons why you should. One, it's a full moon tonight and it's nothing like you've ever seen before, up in the mountains." He paused and wrapped his hands around her waist, pulling her closer to him, making Madison forget just why she should be saying no to this, instead of begging to sign up.

"And two, if you come with us, we'll fuck you so hard under the stars you'll think you're in outer space."

Her breath hitched. It shouldn't have. The line was stupid and the bribery obvious. But her desire for both of these men had grown nothing but stronger in the few days they'd been sleeping together, as had her sexual curiosity.

You're allowed to want this, Madison. There is nothing wrong with taking what you want.

"I don't have a sleeping bag." Her voice came out squeaky and Ryder's eyes clouded over with a hint of desire. She liked it, liked inspiring a reaction in this unflappable man, even as he stood before her, so powerful and strong and capable. Having been accustomed to being the one in control, Madison enjoyed using it for something other than work or responsibilities. Though they were the ones dominating her — her body and her mind — she had just as much power and ability to control them, if she worked it right.

"Not that we're planning on doing much sleeping," Ryder said on a growl, "but we've got extras. Now, grab what you need and come meet us downstairs in five minutes."

Madison winced. She hadn't even packed for a trip to the *dentist* in five minutes, let alone an overnight camping adventure. Ryder knew that.

"And if I take longer?" She put her hands on her hips and tilted her head to look him in those dangerously blue eyes. "Then what?"

He took a step closer to her, his gaze heavy and blazing, and Madison resisted the urge to step back. At the expression on his face, her nipples tightened and her pussy clenched, already throbbing in anticipation of what was to come, and, she hoped, sooner than tonight.

"Sugar, if it takes you longer than five minutes to pack then you're taking too much." Another step forward. "And as for that mouth of yours, I've got a few ideas for dealing with that." He wrapped his hand around her hip to keep her from getting any farther away—not that Madison really wanted to—and grinned down at her. God, his smile made her think of whipped cream and summer nights and all the different ways *dessert* could be interpreted.

"Like what?"

"Like this." He backed her against the wall and held her arms tight over her head. Fuck, but the idea of being at his complete mercy made her hot and turned her body molten in his hands, images of silk scarves and headboards crossing her mind. Ryder bent down and devoured her mouth, using his tongue to explore her, taste her, tease her, until Madison whimpered and begged against his lips, arching into him, riding the thick bulge behind his denim.

Then he pulled back, taking a step away from her until there was too much distance between them for her to touch him anymore.

"Five minutes," he said. And he was out of the door before she could call his name.

In the end, Maddy didn't pop her head down the stairs for fifteen minutes, but it was less than he'd been expecting. He should have known better than to tease her. After all, a mere few days on a ranch was not going to wash away the city dust. But he had seen changes in her—slight, small details that she might not have even realized, ones that showed some of the ranch life was seeping into her blood and turning her a little wild. He looked forward to seeing just *how* wild.

Fifteen minutes or not, Maddy had managed to pack a duffel bag so full that he had to wonder if she'd gone out to the store and bought more stuff. She dropped it on the table and the sound of creaking wood echoed through the kitchen.

Ryder raised an eyebrow. "How'd you fit the bathtub in a bag that size?" he asked.

Maddy scowled. "I haven't been camping since college," she sniped. "I didn't know what I'd need."

He eyed the zipped bag. "Not that…" He unzipped it and pulled out a pair of flip-flops and dropped them on the chair. Next, a swimsuit. *Chair.* Two sweaters. *Chair. Chair.* An extra pair of jeans. *Chair.* A bag of makeup.

"Jesus, Maddy, we're going into the woods, not doing a photo-shoot for an L.L. Bean catalog. You need a toothbrush, a sweatshirt and a water bottle."

She pouted and he pulled her close, enjoying the way her bottom lip jutted out, tempting and teasing him, making his cock surge. He thought about her lips around him, sucking him deep and hard. The pout turned to something else, something more wicked and dangerous when he brushed against her.

"Won't you keep me warm tonight?" she asked him, blinking those pretty brown eyes up at him. The sight gave his heart a strange shuddering vibration that Ryder didn't quite know what to do with.

"Oh, I plan on it," he said. "Keeping you warm has become my favorite pastime." And if he didn't want to delve too deep into why that was, well, fuck it.

"If you two are quite finished making sex eyes at each other," Christian said, walking through the backdoor, "we better hit the road while we've still got good light."

He stopped, eyeing the enormous spread of Madison's stuff all over the kitchen chairs. "You're kidding, city girl." Oh, yeah, no way was she full Montana yet.

"Ryder's only letting me bring three things," she said. "So don't worry about it. Need me to move the car so we can take the truck?" They both laughed and she sighed. "We're hiking, aren't we?"

"Hence the reason you're only allowed three things," Ryder said. "We've got food packed and a charger for the phones. Modern day camping does involve communication in case of emergency."

"Noted." She yanked a UCLA sweatshirt from the depths of her ever-expanding bag before walking over the fridge and grabbing her water bottle from the second self. "Am I allowed toothpaste to go with my toothbrush, or do I have to scavenge for wild mint?"

Ryder laughed. She was quick and he liked that, liked that she gave as well as she got, that she didn't take anything sitting down, not even their ribbing.

"We'll take the toothpaste," he said. "Come on, let's hit the road."

Because it felt a little odd to talk about sharing toothpaste with her, and because the idea that the woman he'd thought to be the picture perfect city girl was weaseling her way into his life, even after just a few days, made him uncomfortable.

Sure, he had people in his life he cared about. Christian, obviously, and Bill, who had practically adopted Ryder at sixteen. He had cared so much about Mason, too, the sting of his loss far deeper and more painful than anything he'd felt after his own father's death. But when was the last time he'd allowed himself to care for a woman — *really* care for a woman? Never.

Not once had he found someone who he pictured any sort of future with. And that was terrifying.

So he grabbed his sleeping bag from the mud room, his hunting rifle—just as a precaution—and a bag of necessities, before heading outside. Right now, he needed a little fresh air to clear his head, or he would start believing the dangerous kind of things his mind kept telling him—*you like her.*

Chapter Ten

The hike wasn't that bad, truth be told. In a former life, Madison had hiked on the weekends, driving out from UCLA to Sequoia National Park for an afternoon of swimming or exploring with her roommates. Back before work had taken over her life and her weekends, she'd enjoyed the great outdoors—in small doses, at least.

And the stretch in her legs and fresh air on her face was only improved by the company she kept. Even in the quiet of their walk, she felt safe and comfortable around these two men in a way she hadn't in a long time. They didn't need to talk, not to settle into their walking ease, and she liked that, liked knowing they were there. Even after just a few days, she felt calmer and more relaxed around them than she had around Joshua in a long time.

Not that Joshua had any business edging into her life now.

You're going to need to face up to him at some point, Madison. You need to come to terms with this.

With what? With the hurt and ache and *embarrassment* of finding her fiancé with another woman in their bed just over a week ago? Hell, she hadn't even told Lily about this, and she'd told Lily everything, from crushes to work problems to getting into college. Lily knew most things about Madison's life before she knew them. But the idea of telling her best friend the truth about her relationship made that familiar ache in her chest pang hard and rough. Of course, Lils wouldn't judge, but Madison just didn't feel like being on display like that, not with something she should have known so much better about.

"We're here." Ryder pushed through a few more trees and into a small clearing, where the forest gave way to a great expanse of sky and mountain. The sun just edged over the horizon, casting long, glowing strands against the sky in burning orange and saccharine pink. Already, pinpoints of stars were glowing out from the soft purple of twilight and Madison knew more were to come. Hell, the stars on her ceiling as a kid had been more than San Francisco ever got, what with the pollution and smog. No doubt Montana would be amazing.

And that was all the more reason she shouldn't have come, even with the promise of mind-blowing sex. This place called to her, made her want to do insane, absurd, wild things — made her want to quit her job and leave the city where she'd spent her entire life, except for college, in. Hell, she'd never lived outside California.

She tossed her sleeping bag on the ground and watched Christian start a fire in the small circle they'd used before, if she was any judge. The problem was, it would be way too easy for her to get used to a life like this—then what? These guys were nothing more to her—and she was nothing more to them—than a fling. That was it. She was going and they were staying and there was nothing more to it than that.

"Come sit by me, sugar." Ryder patted the spot on his sleeping bag between his muscled thighs. She settled in, enjoying the strength of his chest against her back, loving how she felt warm and protected and comfortable in his embrace, watching Christian set up the fire before them.

"Have either of you ever dated a woman?" she asked, wishing at once she could shove the question back into her mouth when it was out. But it was too late, so she continued, hoping for the best. "I mean, this whole thing, do you only sleep with women together or..."

Christian's eyes held humor as he settled on his sleeping bag beside her. Ryder's chest rumbled behind her with a soft laugh.

"We've definitely dated before, on our *own*." Christian pulled a bottle of whiskey from the pack and unscrewed it. "But it's not an easy lifestyle. We work hard and often and most women deserve more time than we can give them."

Madison didn't like the ache in her chest at his words.

"With our hours and our workload," Ryder put in, "we could go days or weeks without leaving the ranch. Town is forty minutes away and the next closest residence is six miles down the road. So the relationships don't always work out."

Christian smiled and handed her the whiskey bottle. "They never work out. It's no one's fault—I'm not going to go around saying I've got a crazy ex-girlfriend or anything. The women I dated just wanted to spend more time with me than I could give them and it wasn't fair. That's pretty much it."

She liked that answer. Christian was right on the money with the crazy ex comment, since so many men demonized the women they had dated as a way of playing victim. But being in a relationship took trust and love and respect, and unwillingness to give that meant a person didn't get to play the victim. Unless, of course, that person's fiancé was a shitbag.

"And this whole sleeping-with-one-woman thing?" she asked, curiosity winning out over the need to harp on Joshua anymore. "What's that about?"

Ryder shrugged behind her. "Why fix it if it ain't broke?" he asked. "For whatever reason, it works, and we're leaving it at that. Of course, if either of us found the right woman, we'd stop. But for now, we're happy."

She turned and pursed her lips at both of them. "Did you ever..." She pointed between them, making her meaning as clear as she could. Ryder, who'd been swallowing a sip of whiskey, choked hard.

His eyes watered and he hacked again before answering, "Nope. We've somehow managed to avoid that."

Christian looked a lot less disconcerted. "Eh, I can't say I never thought about. I mean, I've seen this guy naked more times that I've seen any woman naked, but it just doesn't do it for me." He accepted the whiskey bottle and drank a slow sip. "Plus, if I was into guys, I'd want someone with a bigger dick."

Ryder flipped him off and Christian just grinned, the devil in his smile, before handing the whiskey bottle back to Madison.

"What about you, city girl?" he asked. "Do you have a husband back at home? Two kids and a dog? Are we your dirty little secret?"

This time, *she* choked on the whiskey, laughing and tearing up. "Well, I haven't told anyone about this," she said. "But I definitely don't have a husband. Or a dog. I don't have time for either of them, apparently."

The air around them grew still and she realized that her voice had gone bitter. It was here. The reckoning of what she'd walked in on last week had come. And there wasn't a damn thing she could do about it.

"All right, you've danced around this before and now you need to fess up," Ryder said, stroking her arm with a gentle, soothing stroke. "What the hell happened that has you all twisted in knots?" The tone of his voice and the fire in Christian's eyes promised Madison that she had allies in these two men. And really, who better to tell her tale of woe than strangers in a far-off place? Lily would no doubt get into her car and drive to Joshua's apartment with every intention of teaching him a lesson, and Madison just didn't want that.

"Do I have to?" She took the whiskey bottle out of Ryder's hands and cradled it in her own, as a safety net.

"Looks like you want to," Christian replied. "We're good listeners."

Yeah, she knew that. She also knew they were great lovers, hard workers and both whip-smart. The last thing any of them needed was her divulging more secrets, giving yet another reason for intimacy and connection. But she *did* want to talk about it, because it had been weighing so heavy on her chest that she felt fit to burst, anger ricocheting through her veins.

"All right…" She drank long from the whiskey bottle before beginning. "I found out about the ranch on

Wednesday last week, right?" They both nodded. "Yeah, well, Monday of last week I found my fiancé in bed with his law partner. *Our* bed."

There. She had said it out loud to other people. And that had been the part that had scared her the most. Once she said it out loud, it was true. Once she said it out loud, there was no going back to the life she had lived before this week. She would go home to half an apartment, to a job that had sounded the death knell for her relationship, to no one.

"Son of a bitch," Christian muttered, each word torn off in barely veiled rage. "Maddy, you give us the word and we'll drive all night to go kick his ass."

Ryder's whole body had stiffened behind her and she could almost taste his potent anger. Their advocacy and rage on her behalf vindicated her own and Madison could at last smile about the whole situation for the first time since it'd happened.

"Oh, don't worry about that," she said. Both men narrowed their eyes at her.

"What'd you do, Maddy?" Ryder asked, clenching his hands in a gesture of possession around her waist. *Oh, I could so get used to this.*

"I put his Rolex in the blender," she said, unable to contain her mirth at the confession. "The scream was pretty satisfying."

"It'd be more satisfying for me to put my boot in his face," Ryder replied. "But I like the way you think." He bent and kissed the back of her neck, soft, reassuring, perhaps not intended to be anything more than that, but she still felt the heat of him down to her bones, aching and rioting through her with a promise of want and anticipation and need.

"I'm okay," she said, believing it for the first time since her suspicions had been confirmed. "Or, at least, I will be. He said I worked too hard and that he never got to see me, which is why he *strayed,* but it was really only a matter of time. I'm just glad it happened before we got married. That would have sucked major ass." She sighed, feeling the intense urge to tell them everything, to explain just what it was that had apparently driven Joshua away from her.

"He said I was a freak. In bed, I mean," she said at last, looking first Christian then Ryder in the eye. "He said I wanted things that normal women didn't want. In the end, he really wasn't a nice guy. I was just the last one to notice."

Ryder kissed the back of her neck, but even the gentle touch held a note of ill-suppressed anger.

"He's a bastard," he said, low and hot. "If there's anything we've learned from our own thing here, Madison, it's that communication and trust are necessary for sex and love. He should never have made you feel bad about yourself for having different desires than he did. There's nothing wrong with you."

To her horror, Madison's eyes got hot. Jesus *fuck,* when was the last time she had cried over a man? Not since her college boyfriend had transferred to NYU during their senior year.

"I know that," she said, her throat a little tight. "Rationally, I know he treated the situation — treated *me* all wrong. It's just hard to believe it. In the end, I'm still the fool here."

Ryder hugged her closer to him and Christian took both of her hands in his, his temper simmering hot and potent below the surface. On a good day, Christian looked a little raw, a little angry and a lot of scary, with the tattoos and the piercings. But right now, against the light of the fire and the stark moon, he looked as though he could kill Joshua if Madison gave him the word. Not that she ever would, but the knowledge was a little comforting — or maybe it was just knowing that she wasn't so alone in all this, and that other men — sexy as hell and totally demanding other men — liked all the parts of her Joshua hadn't.

Diving into this affair had been what she'd needed to remember herself under all the pain and hurt that the betrayal and his words had caused. Or maybe she had just needed Ryder and Christian.

"Have you told anyone else about this?" Christian asked in a quiet voice, while he stroked her hand. "Or have you been holding it in this whole time?"

Madison sucked on her teeth then reached for the whiskey bottle and downed a healthy drink before replying. "I guess I didn't want to tell anyone because once I said it out loud, that made it true, you know? I'll talk to Lily when I get home, but I'm not looking forward to that conversation. It was easier to tell you guys first, for whatever reason." *It's the same reason that I'm scared to spend too much time with them, because I know I could fall for both of these guys, hard, if I haven't already.*

"I'm glad you told us," Ryder said, still planting those damn kisses up and down her neck, turning her to mush. "I hate the idea of you suffering through this alone."

She turned her head and kissed him, hard. "I'm not alone," she said. "And you've both been awesome with the whole distraction thing. Plus, the timing on the inheritance really kept me from thinking about it too much until this weekend."

Christian picked up her hand kissed the inside of her wrist. "Will you let us distract you now?" he asked. "Let us take your mind off things?"

Madison smirked. Damn it, they were already getting to her, with the smirking and the teasing and all of it and she couldn't deny for a second that she liked it.

"You can try," she challenged, shooting him a wink. Yeah, fuck Joshua and fuck what he'd done to her. The only good part was that she'd learned the truth of who he was before it was too late. *And that I got the chance to meet Christian and Ryder…*

Ryder's kisses grew longer and more languid and he ran his teeth down her back, slowly, tantalizingly, until Madison's breath got shallow, her nipples peaked and she threw her head back against his shoulder. Christian kissed her then, a slow, deep, promising kiss that said so much more than desire. It spoke of camaraderie and friendship and support and promises of a night spent out under the stars doing what most people only considered a fantasy. She pressed back into the kiss, moaning against his lips and rocking into Ryder's hardness just behind her ass.

The sensations overwhelmed her. She had never felt this way before and she never would again, not with any other lover, at least. Even simple kisses, brushes of lips across neck and collarbone, made her ache with a need so acute her mind blanked, her vision blurred and her pussy clenched on emptiness.

"I need… I need…" she whispered against Christian's mouth, shuddering when Ryder brought his hands to her breasts and began teasing her peaked nipples. Her nipples had always been sensitive, and when he was the one touching them they zinged with electricity, each rough caress making her arch and moan and quake.

"What do you need?" Christian slipped his hand below the hem of her shirt and up her ribcage, soft, sweet caresses that made her moan and whimper. "Tell us, Maddy. Tell us what you want." Like the bastard didn't know.

"I want you…" she managed, and a wild, insane image popped into her head — having them both *inside* her at the same time. "I want someone to *touch* me." Her voice came out ragged and demanding. Jesus, only a few hours had passed since she'd last had them inside her and already she was running hot, desperate and willing to beg for what she wanted.

"How, baby?" Ryder murmured into her ear. "Tell us *how* you want us. What's going through that pretty little head?"

She couldn't tell them *that*. Not when the ideas running roughshod over her mind were so insane and perverse and…

"Don't go there, Madison. We're not your ex and we don't ever want you to hold back on what you want because of things he said to you." Frustration at her pain was back in Christian's voice, stark and uncovered. "What we're doing right now is about trust and communication — if anything doesn't feel right for any of us, we stop. You have to believe we want something unless we tell you otherwise, okay?"

She hadn't realized she'd needed those words until he said them, hadn't realized that Joshua's dismissal of even her tamer desires had pulled at a heartstring, had put a distance between them that might just have led to the extra-late hours she'd worked and the weekend projects she had taken on. But now, as the two men touched and kissed and gazed at her under a blanket of stars so rich in diamond lights that she felt a little magical, Madison realized how important it was for her be honest, with them, but more so with herself, especially now.

"I want to have you both inside," she whispered. Knowing she wanted it, had to say it, didn't mean it was easy and she hesitated a bit, never having voiced the words out loud. Hell, Joshua had run scared at the idea of tying her to the headboard — never in a million years would she have broached this one.

"You've had us both, baby," Ryder whispered, realization dawning in his voice. "Ahhh… You have to say it, Maddy. You have to tell us what you want. Take your control back and trust us." And Jesus, for better or for worse, she did trust them, probably too much for her own good.

"I want to try anal. I've experimented by myself before, but never with a partner and I want to know how it feels to have you both in me at the same time. You can say no." The words came out in a tumble, but she felt lighter, freer in this wide-open air, with her desires on full display. The worst they could say was no, but at least she'd have admitted to herself what she wanted and that was a damn big step to getting over everything Joshua had done and said.

"Jesus, Maddy…" Christian's voice came out on a groan and her stomach plummeted for a half-second. *He's going to say he doesn't want it, he's going to say there's something wrong with me… Joshua was right, most normal women don't want this kind of thing…*

"Do you know how badly I want that? We want that? We didn't want to push you before you were ready, baby, but I have been fantasizing about burying my cock in your ass ever since you showed up in that goddamn tight skirt."

Madison laughed, relief flooding through her. Joshua hadn't been right about her, and even as she knew the truth of it, hearing that someone else shared her desires soothed her aching heart like a balm. Action on instinct, she pressed forward and kissed all of her tangled emotions into Christian's mouth, exploring, tasting, demanding, until he took over the kiss, took over her, palming one breast and nipping at her tongue, her lips, her jaw. She moaned, grinding back against Ryder's cock just when Christian slipped his tongue between her lips and tasted her.

"So fucking responsive," Christian growled when he pulled back from her mouth to nip at her collarbone. "I want to fulfill your fantasies, Maddy. Jesus, I'll do whatever the hell you want me to. Just say the word."

She couldn't help herself. She laughed into his kiss. "I do have a cock ring I've been wanting to try." To Christian's credit, he didn't freak out, but she put him out of his misery before he had to come up with an excuse. "I'm kidding!" She turned around to kiss Ryder. "I'd much prefer to relinquish control than take it. I'm responsible for everything else in my life and I like it a lot more when you two are in charge instead."

"Then let us be in charge, Maddy," Ryder whispered against her ear, moving their bodies slow and easy so she lay flat against the sleeping bag, both of them hovering over her. The sight was intimating—two large, powerful men giving her beyond sexy grins—but to Madison, the moment couldn't have been more full of trust or comfort. *Funny how that all goes.*

"If you need us to stop, you say stop," Ryder continued. "We're doing something tonight you've never done before and we need you to know you can trust us."

She reached up and stroked his face then turned to Christian and smiled. "I trust you both completely. You've already made me feel more at ease than my fiancé ever did. But yes, if something doesn't feel right, I promise I'll let you know." The concern vanished from both their gazes, at once replaced by a fiery, potent lust that made her squeeze her legs tight. Her nipples pebbled and she groaned. "Now, can we get to the fun part?"

"Those are my favorite words," Christian growled. "With the exception of, *yes, Christian, harder*, but we'll get to that." He scooted down her legs to untie her boots and toss them to the side, along with her socks.

Ryder kissed the inside of her neck, pressing soft heat to her collarbone and jaw, as he explored her ribs and stomach with his hand. He brushed the underside of her breast and Madison bowed, arching up into his touch and murmuring under her breath. Already her nipples swelled with need and her pussy ached, tightening when Christian ran his hand up her leg and across the band of her jeans.

"Teases," she growled. "Both of you are horrible teases."

"You're giving us control," Ryder reminded her, but he lifted her back a bare inch to help yank the T-shirt over her head. Then, kissing her hard, he set about unhooking her bra and tossing the underwear off to the side. Within seconds, her breasts were bare, nipples pointing up to the clear blue sky.

Ryder leaned down and took one nipple into his mouth, running his teeth gently against the swollen tip. She bucked, giving Christian the chance to tug her now-unbuttoned jeans down her hips. Madison searched for purchase as Ryder continued to tease her, grabbing on to the synthetic fabric of the sleeping bag when he rolled her other nipple between two rough fingers.

Christian pulled her jeans off the rest of the way then looked down to admire her from his perch at the foot of the sleeping bag.

"I like the blue on you, city girl." He snapped one of the thin strips of lace that made up her thong. "I'd like it more off you, though." He admired her for another moment before lifting her hips off the ground and sliding the lace down her legs. Then he spread her knees wide and looked down at her, eyes hungry and smile promising. "You already wet, Maddy?" he asked. "Does talking about your fantasies turn you on? Because if you ever need someone to listen you to list them off, I'm right here." He slipped one finger down the line of her legs, hovering just at her wet entrance, teasing, tempting. She tried to move, to take him deeper into her body, but Ryder placed his hands on her hips and held her still.

"Give us control, Maddy," he said. "Let us make you feel good."

She nodded, and a small moan escaped her lips at the look in Ryder's eyes. Then a larger moan, when Christian slid first one, then two, then three fingers deep inside her, pulsing just that little bit. She bucked, the action demanding and involuntary, trying to take more of him, but Christian just shook his head.

"We're going slow," he said. "Can you get up on your knees for me, baby?"

Ryder moved out of her way and Madison turned over onto her hands and knees, her legs trembling a little in anticipation and excitement, more so when she felt Christian's deep gaze upon her, inspecting her, examining her from behind. To her left, Ryder fumbled with the bag and pulled out a handful of condoms and a bottle of lube. He tossed a condom and the small bottle to Christian, then yanked his T-shirt off his head before kicking off his boots.

Behind her, Christian did the same and Madison just waited, her anticipation building and making her ache in heavier desperation with every passing moment. Then Ryder slid under her belly and leaned up, pressing heated kisses to her aching clit before slipping his tongue between her folds and deep into her pussy. She screamed, her fingers digging into the fabric below her until she was rocking against his mouth. His touch was so distracting that she almost didn't notice the finger pressing against her tighter hole until Christian leaned down to whisper in her ear.

"Just relax, baby," he murmured. "I promise I'll go slow." And he did, easing his finger deep inside her with a slow, careful slide, filling her and stretching her with the single digit. Jesus *Christ*, how the hell was she going to survive both of them inside her at once, if the sensations of Ryder's tongue and Christian's fingers were already driving her to the edge, making her lose control, making her scream and…

Christian slid another slippery finger past her tight ring and she lost it, coming hard against Ryder's mouth and screaming curses to the open night sky, her body trembling and shaking. Slowly, she came down from her high, catching her breath in short pants.

"Jesus, Maddy, you're so fucking tight when you come." Christian's tone ran hot and desperate and she wanted it, all of it. Right now.

"Please…" she murmured, her mind still fuzzy in the wake of her orgasm. "Guys…please."

Ryder grinned up at her when he slid out from under her belly. In record time, he shucked his jeans and slid a condom down his length, the image of him stroking the impressive cock making her mouth water. Then, he lifted her, his hands careful, positioning himself underneath.

"You're in charge, sugar," he said. "Take what you want."

And she did, moving herself down upon his cock in a slow, tantalizing slide, until he bottomed out inside her. She took a deep, long breath, reveling in the way he stretched her body, making her feel full and desired with each pump of his hips.

"You, too," she whispered, turning back around to look at Christian. "Inside me, please."

He nodded, his face serious against the lust, and he slowly slipped one more finger inside her ass, sliding around and stretching her. Even though Madison knew it would be a tight fit, she ached for it, longed for it. Then she got it, when Christian inched his fingers from her ass and fitted his slick, covered cock at her hole.

"Are you ready?" he asked her. Madison just nodded. Christian edged forward, pressing the head of his cock against her. Her body couldn't help tightening but Ryder pressed into her, riding against her swollen clit, and she relaxed, allowing Christian to push through the tight ring of muscle until the tip of his cock rested just inside. Then he pressed forward, inch by agonizing inch. The sensations overwhelmed her, a sense of fullness and heat and pleasure just on the edge of pain, but it didn't hurt, not with the slow and careful pace

Christian kept, until he was buried all the way inside her, balls resting against her ass.

"Jesus *fuck*, Maddy," he growled, his voice carnal and pinched and strung so tightly she thought he might just explode. "You are so fucking tight around my cock, baby. I'm not going to last very long…" Neither was she, not with how tight and stretched she felt then. She just whimpered, and the two men took it as the command it was, moving with slow care inside her. She wanted more. She didn't want slow and she didn't want careful, so she rocked up, taking Christian's cock deep, then Ryder's, then Christian's, then Ryder's, the back and forth driving her higher, each thrust another push toward an overwhelming and insane release.

"That's it, baby," Ryder said, "Take our cocks, ride us… So fucking tight wrapped around me. I love the way you feel…" His words devolved into mumbles, but each curse, each demand sent her higher, got her closer… Ryder leaned up, sucked one of her nipples into his mouth and Madison's orgasm caught her and tossed her right over the edge. She screamed, her pussy and asshole clenching around the two hard cocks buried deep inside her, and she rocked, taking them deeper as she came, screaming and cursing to the open skies.

But when she came down from her high, both cocks were still rock-hard.

"It's too much…" she whispered, even as she felt another orgasm building from the base of her spine, climbing higher, taking her faster and stronger.

"Come with us again, Maddy," Christian demanded. "Come hard around Ryder's dick while I fuck your ass."

The sound that escaped her throat was deep and sinful and Christian groaned. "You like being told what to do, naughty girl." He slapped her fleshy cheek and Madison surged forward. "Well, I like telling you what to do. Keep riding Ryder's cock while I bury my cock in your tight hole. I want you to come hard. I want you to take it while I slap your ass and he bites your nipples."

Then Christian slapped her ass, Ryder sucked one swollen nipple into her mouth and there was nothing left but sheer, insane, overwhelming pleasure. She took and gave as she came, riding hard, her mind registering their two orgasms below and above her as first Ryder then Christian gave in to the pleasure and fell over the edge with trembling, earth-shaking roars.

They collapsed into a heap of tangled limbs against the sleeping bag. Both men pulled out of her body with almost reverent slowness and care and a bone-deep contentment settled into Madison. Ryder leaned over to the bag and grabbed a few tissues. He wiped her body clean and Christian pulled an opened sleeping bag over their naked bodies.

"I don't think I want to leave here," Madison said, looking up to the moon and the brilliant sky.

Ryder took her hand, weaving their fingers together, and Christian snuggled up into the crook of her neck. It was funny how these two so different men continued to surprise her by their actions and their words.

"I don't think we want you to leave here," Christian murmured against her bare skin. "Do we, Ryder?"

Beside her, Ryder shook his head. "No," he said. "I don't think we do."

Sure, she had things to worry about. But right at that moment, with those two gorgeous men fucking her brains out, making her happy in so many different ways, and the wide-open Montana sky lit up with a thousand stars, she couldn't for the life of her remember what those things were.

Chapter Eleven

A sense of innocent giddiness overtook her when Ryder pulled his pickup truck into the makeshift grass parking lot for the Wolf Creek Fourth of July Fair. Even from across the section cut out for parking — which was already more than halfway full — Madison saw a Ferris wheel, several short rollercoasters and three barns lit up in glow lights, almost invisible in the still early afternoon sun. The air was awash in scents, growing stronger the closer they got to the fair — salted, buttery popcorn, fried dough, the bite of grease from old carnival machines and the none too subtle hints of horse manure that she'd found herself surprisingly fond of, these past few days in Wolf Creek.

She'd grown surprisingly fond of a lot, these last few days in Wolf Creek, a town she wouldn't have been able to place on a map of the world until a week ago. Now, she couldn't just place it on a map — she could *place* it, in a real, human, powerful kind of way. Wolf Creek was the ever-present mountain ranges. It was the soft, sweet scents of rushing water. It was fluffy, irritating kittens filled with energy and curiosity. It was the last tie to her mother's past, her past.

It could be her future, too.

Ryder cupped her waist, a light and gentle touch that said so much, before stepping in front of the ticket booth to pay for their admission. As she walked through the open gates, taking in the sights and sounds of the Wolf Creek Fourth of July Fair, Christian's hands brushed her, sending shivers of desire — and something deeper and far more terrifying — racing through her. Just standing there, looking at these two men, her cowboy and her biker, terrified Madison more than any rollercoaster or haunted house. Because this wasn't a trick and she was beginning to realize that it wasn't a game. Not anymore.

Shaking her head of those thoughts, which were distracting, confusing and difficult to unpack, she grabbed both men by the hands and ran, giggling like the kid she hadn't been in almost twenty years, deep into the fairgrounds.

"Do you even know where you're going?" Ryder laughed, his breath catching as they skirted around families, dogs off leashes and a juggler. A few of the more discerning strangers they passed shot her skeptical looks, but Madison didn't care. Coming to terms with her feelings was way too complicated right now, but she damn well deserved the happiness that curled deep inside her when one hand was clutched in Ryder's and the other in Christian's, each strong grip providing comfort and joy that she couldn't explain but needed more of like she needed to breathe.

"It doesn't matter." She released their hands to spin around in a lazy circle, gazing up at the bright blue sky and reveling in the warmth of the summer sun upon her face. When was the last time she had felt so free, so at ease with almost everything? Not at her job, that was for certain, and definitely not with Joshua. But somehow these two men, *together* of all things, made her feel…more than she should.

She stopped short, wanting to laugh out loud at the comical expressions that greeted her when she stumbled a little bit. Both of them reached out to steady her and Madison relaxed into the touch, and the comfort she found there. With them. She leaned up, not caring who saw, to press a kiss to first Christian's mouth then Ryder's. Though each touch of the lips was short, she couldn't deny the barely leashed power behind them, the want both men kept just simmering below the surface. And Madison wanted them back. Right there, in the middle of this county fair, wearing freaking shit kicker boots, she wanted to have sex with two hot-as-hell badass cowboys.

Saying a lot had changed was like saying the Titanic had had a leak. *Everything* had changed.

They toured the fair for hours, stopping at the petting zoo, which just made Ryder grumble about doing work on his days off, a dozen carnival rides, games, market stalls, craft stalls, food stalls, dessert stalls and more. Madison caught a glimpse of a bakery stall down the quiet lane they were walking, at the very far end of the fairgrounds, and filed it away for later, a note she'd need to address when the reality of the idea percolating in her mind finally took purchase.

But for now, instead of thinking about anything else, she was going to focus all her attentions on the two hunks standing beside her. She grabbed each of their hands and squeezed tight before bringing her hands up their hips, one on each side of her. In a fit of joy and overwhelming need to feel that what was happening that day, there, that afternoon, was *real*, she sneaked her hands a little higher and took one handful of hard, muscled ass against each palm.

Christian growled, a full-on, one hundred percent male growl. Ryder let out a laugh that ran rough with lust and the dragging, carnal sounds made her nipples pebble behind the soft white cotton of her shirt, aching to be touched.

"You're going to have to learn to keep your hands to yourself, city girl," Christian whispered, brushing a stray hair from her face, where the wind — or wandering hands — had swept it.

Madison grinned up at him and arched an eyebrow. "Or what?"

Ryder pinched her ass, his face not at all apologetic when she turned to glare at him.

"Or we'll take you into the abandoned barn over by the stables and have our way with you a few hundred yards from everyone in Wolf Creek," he said, dragging her by the hand into a small, hidden alcove behind a tree. "Unless that's what you were going for."

Her breath caught a little, tangled in a mix of excitement and desire. Would she ever stop wanting either of these guys? *Not a snowball's chance in hell.* She wanted them both naked and under her, on top of her, on both sides of her, from the moment she woke up in the morning to the minute after she fell asleep at night. Judging by the way they both seemed to be holding her closer now, the tension simmering between them, they ached for her with just as much intensity.

"Are we interrupting something?" A deep, male voice broke through her lusty haze and she looked up, aware of the nearness of both men, hovering just above her. Two more men stood before them, in their little alcove off the main dirt path of the fair.

"You know damn well you're interrupting something, Deckard," the second man said. Christian and Ryder kept close, even as they moved to embrace the men.

"Sons of bitches," Ryder said. "Maddy, this is Micah Ellison." He pointed to the man who had spoken second in a quiet and far more subdued tone. He was Native American, large and sinewy, whose powerful muscles were not hidden by the simple gray T-shirt he wore. His hair was long, much longer than hers, and ink black, shimmery and beautiful. He curved full lips into a half-smile and nudged the guy beside him.

"This nosy bastard is Dec McCormick," he said, extending his hand to her. "We work search and rescue in the mountains, so we're not around much, but we couldn't miss the fair."

"Madison Hollis," she said, accepting his handshake, then Dec's. Dec was tall, though not quite as tall as Micah, his short brown hair and light green eyes another contrast. "It's nice that you guys could get down for a little while, though. I've only been out here a few days, but I can imagine it gets lonely in the mountains, beautiful as they are."

Dec shrugged, a mischievous expression on his face. She knew he was all kinds of trouble, but she sort of liked that. It seemed Wolf Creek was full of all sorts of trouble.

"Not if you know where to find good company," he said with a wink.

Micah rolled his eyes. "You intentionally interrupted a grope-fest to flirt?" he asked, in the way only a person who'd known someone forever could do. "I'm not getting involved if these two decide to kick your ass. You'd deserve it." He turned to Madison. "What brings you to Wolf Creek, Ms. Hollis?" Behind the polite question, there was curiosity in his eyes, and more of that Montana Men trouble she seemed to find around every turn.

"We'd appreciate your...discretion," she began, her voice hesitant, "about the grope-fest, I mean."

Ryder and Christian both stiffened beside her, but when she turned to look at them, they were stifling laughs. *Trouble and sons of bitches. All of them.*

Dec shrugged and somehow even that simple motion was laden with swagger.

"Whatever's in your teacup, ma'am, I wasn't put on this earth to judge."

She nodded, unable to keep the small smile from forming on her face. "Thanks. And to answer your question, I recently inherited Triple Diamond Ranch, actually. Christian and Ryder and I have been figuring the best way to move forward with the ranch, now that my uncle is gone."

Micah's eyes went soft. "We are sorry to hear of your loss, Ms. Hollis. Mason was a good man. The community will miss him."

She nodded, appreciating how Wolf Creek seemed to be the family to Mason she'd never had to the opportunity to be. A brief quiet stretched, then it seemed to register for both men and they spoke at the same time.

"You inherited the ranch?"

"*Triple Diamond.*"

"You're the one..."

After a moment, they settled down and looked in expectation at her. Madison just shrugged, a self-effacing grin breaking across her face.

"The guys got me out of the stilettos and into the shit kickers, so I'd say I'm well on my way," she said with a smile. At that, she felt a sharp pinch on her ass. Then another. Unsure of who had their hands snaked around her back—or rather, which one of them, she kept a straight face and smiled at Dec and Micah. "It's definitely different out here from San Francisco."

She coughed when one hand sneaked around and slipped just that little bit under her cotton skirt.

"We're technically located on your land then, ma'am," Micah said. "Our team does search and rescue from a compound in the mountains, about two miles from Holmwood."

Dec raised an eyebrow. "I've never had a landlady fantasy before. I'm sure I could come up with something."

Madison almost laughed out loud when Ryder and Christian puffed out their chests. She didn't doubt for a second that Dec was egging them on. The grin in his eyes said he'd flirt with a table, long as it had at least two legs, but there was humor too and she felt perfectly comfortable around both him and Micah. That Christian and Ryder seemed to be getting possessive was something to consider, however...

In fact... Ryder kissed her first, fierce and demanding and very much a statement. The second she was able to get her breath back, Christian kissed her too, gripping her waist in his big fingers and making her sigh and lean back against Ryder's hard body.

"Told you we interrupted something," Micah said, nudging Dec in the gut. He shot Madison a knowing, humor-laced smile. "Y'all be safe now. We'll catch you guys later. Dec wanted to see if there were any dogs we could grab at the adoption tent and you look…busy."

"It was nice to meet you," Madison called after them, but they didn't turn around. Even she couldn't deny the incredible flush running up her face and across the mounds of her swollen breasts.

"Dec may talk a mile a minute, but he knows when to keep his mouth shut." Christian took her hand and pulled her into the empty barn, Ryder close on her heels. "Especially since we all know those two get up to stuff in the mountains. Not *together*," he clarified, when she shot him an amused look. "But Dec's got a reputation. Micah less so, though, who's to say for sure? I've lived in the same town as both those guys pretty much my whole life and I could sum up what I actually know about Micah in about three sentences."

They'd walked while they spoke and within a few minutes came to the far end of the barn. Though the building was close to the edge of the fairground, the sound was muted just outside its walls, even more so when Christian led them into one stall that smelled of fresh hay and was deserted.

"Will anyone find us here?" Madison asked, more because she kind of felt like she should than anything else. For whatever reason, having Dec and Micah know the truth of what was between them and not giving a damn about it somehow validated that whatever existed between her and Christian and Ryder was really happening. She wouldn't wake up in her empty apartment in downtown San Fran, remembering the feeling of two strong, work-roughened men loving her. No, she'd wake on a cloud in a beautiful hand-built house, feeling two work-roughened men loving her. She'd take option two any day of the week.

"Does it matter?" Ryder asked.

Madison shook her head, feeling that familiar thrill she got when the two of them stalked over to her like hungry jungle cats spying their prey. Very willing prey. Because she had slept with Christian and Ryder alone, and while she ached with different, deep, needy parts of herself for those moments spent alone, being with the two of them together was unlike anything she had ever known before, or would ever know again.

"I dunno. I think you liked that those guys knew." Christian pinned her against the wooden wall. "I think it turns you on a little bit that we could be discovered at any moment. Greedy girl. Two isn't enough?"

She yanked him down for a hard kiss, his words and his mouth making her mind fuzzy and desperation bloom within her, aching to be fed.

"You two are enough," she said, the honesty raw in her voice. "I don't want this with anyone else. Just you two."

So what if the words tasted a little tangy on her tongue? They needed to be said.

"Oh, sugar..." Ryder leaned down and kissed her, soft and slow and so beautiful in a way that made her toes tingle and her spine bow, pressing her forward into both large men standing just in front of her. "You're awful hard to say no to when you put it like that."

Madison looked up to him, his gaze a little wild and a lot intense. Christian's was too, just this side of unhinged and already making her body surge and quake, trembling with unspent need.

"Then say yes."

She loved that look. They both had it, though just like with everything between these men there were subtle differences. Ryder's eyes got a little dark, from sapphire to midnight blue, pulling away the curtain of his pretty boy package to reveal a little of the more intense man beneath. Christian took on the predatory gaze of a hungry jaguar, ready to play with his prey before he pounced, because he had no doubt he'd be the victor. Either way, either man, that *look* meant she was about six seconds from being bent over the nearest flat surface.

"How about we make you scream it, instead?" Christian moved one hand in a possessive slide under her skirt until he met with bare ass. "Fuck me running, city girl—if I'd known you'd been walking around without panties on all day, I've have thrown you over my shoulder and carried you off like a damn caveman."

Madison shot him a look that she knew was redolent with smug devilry. It seemed that just a few days in the company of her hot cowboys had her throwing caution and politeness to the wind in favor of something a lot more fun.

Not my cowboys.

She enjoyed that they wanted her as much as she wanted them. "You've got me now…"

Christian pressed his hard body into her back, his cock surging against her ass when he rolled his hips. Before her, Ryder cupped her head and claimed her mouth in a possessive, overwhelming display. If Madison didn't know any better, she'd say that both of them kind of liked that Dec and Micah knew the score.

But then she wasn't thinking anymore, because Christian dropped to his knees, flipped her skirt up and pressed his mouth to her pussy in the span of three seconds. She surged forward and Ryder caught her in his strong embrace, kissing her with deep, languid touches that made her skin burn. She shut her eyes, dragging her lip into her mouth to stifle the overwhelming need to scream, and squeezed his arms. Christian continued his slow, teasing assault, sliding his tongue in and out of her hole until she was fisting Ryder's shirt and riding Christian's mouth.

Ryder slid his mouth from hers, placing heated, promising kisses to her neck, to her collarbone, to the bulging, swollen mounds of her breasts in the cotton shirt that had *somehow* fallen down past decent. He freed one breast from her shirt and bra and sucked her straining nipple into his mouth.

She surged forward, unable to think, to react, to do anything but feel the onslaught of sensations as both Ryder and Christian kissed and sucked and took her in their talented mouths. Then, as fast as she had risen, she peaked, catching her heights of pleasure in a moment of blinding light and need and want and she did scream that time, riding both men until the tremors of her release overtook her and she collapsed against Ryder's chest.

"Damn, sugar," Ryder said on a low growl. "Someone might think you're not getting enough at home."

She laughed, the sound ragged and husky. "Am I still alive?" she asked. Ryder grinned and Christian pinched her ass. He stood from his position between her legs.

"We're just getting started," he whispered in her ear. He brought his strong hand to her hair and dragged her face to his, where their mouths collided in pleasure and want and promises.

"I don't think I'm going to survive," she whispered, when Christian broke off. "But sign me up for going out this way."

Christian chuckled, his strong hand guiding her head forward until she was bent over, her head just level with Ryder's cock, throbbing behind taut denim. *Mmm, I like how these men think.* Especially since Christian's fingers were now exploring her ass, exposed by the position and much to his liking, if the thick, promising squeeze he gave to one cheek was anything to go by.

"What do you want, Maddy?" Ryder asked, looking down on her. She could get way too accustomed to a position like this, heady, needy eyes following her every move, waiting for her to take control. Because, despite being wedged between the two of them in a barn with a thousand people just outside, Madison knew just who had control here and she was going to take every advantage of it.

"I want you both inside me," she said, "just like this, filling me from both ends. I want you to give in, not to hold back..." She paused, a little self-conscious. "I think I like it rough."

Ryder's eyebrows went up, but his expression changed to one of interest and concern. For her. The lust gone, he stroked her hair, his rough, calloused hand following the line of her cheek.

"Are you sure?" His fingers never wavered in their soft touch. "You don't have to give us anything. There's nothing here to prove."

Madison shook her head. "I'm not...I'm not trying to prove anything, I just want you to take control, both of you. Right now I want to feel you and feel marked by you. I'm giving in."

Deep in her heart, Madison knew full well that those words weren't just about sex or pleasure or even trust. They were so much more dangerous than that.

But for now, she had something a lot more delicious to focus her attention on, so she pressed back against Christian's swollen dick and brought deft hands up to Ryder's fly, undoing the zipper and button with as much speed as she could, before raising an eyebrow at him.

"I'm waiting," she said, though there was no denying the slight hitch in her voice.

"Well, we can't have that, now can we?" Christian unwrapped a condom, the telltale crinkling echoing in the empty room. He brushed his covered cock across her ass, lightly slapping the top of one of the mounds, before rubbing it against her wet slit.

And oh *god*, she was wet. Her early orgasm had been insane, but the maleness of them standing in front of and behind her, the expressions in their eyes and the heat radiating off both their bodies made her skin burn for touch and her heart ache, desire pooling in every spare space across her entire body.

In front of her, Ryder freed his cock from the confines of his jeans, slowly stroking it, the hardness already pulsing just a breath too far from her mouth. Her expression must have changed, because Ryder let out a low laugh.

"I could get off just watching you pout," he said, the honesty raw in his voice. "But I'd much rather have you touch too. How about a little begging for my cock in your mouth, baby? I wanna hear just how much you want." He stopped stroking for a beat. "You do want it, don't you?"

Her pout got deeper. "Yes, I want it." Son of bitch knew exactly what she wanted. They both did and they had somehow decided that neither of them had any intention of giving it to her until she had lost her goddamn mind. Behind her, Christian's tip rested just too far away from her entrance, so close but nowhere near filling her the way she ached and needed and longed to be filled.

"Please…"

Ryder cocked one eyebrow, which said everything he was clearly thinking without words. Madison tried again. "I wanna suck you." A little of her own honesty slipped into the words, raw, desperate, willing to do whatever it took to get him inside of her. Both of them. "Please, Sir, can I suck your dick?"

That seemed to suit him a little better, and he palmed the crown of his seeping cock against her lips. The salty musk of him tanged against her mouth and tongue and a surge of wetness spilled from between her thighs.

"Sir," Christian said, pulling her thoughts away from Ryder's cock, just for a moment. "I like sir. Can you sir me?"

She nodded, darting her tongue out to brush Ryder's slit and enjoying the hiss of pleasure he made.

"Please, *Sir*, will you fill my cunt?" Another fucking tease, as he slid his hardness just across her wet opening, nowhere near to being enough contact. She let out a low string of curses and tried to move forward or back, but strong hands on both her shoulders and waist kept her in place.

"Such a desperate, wet little thing," Ryder groaned. "Shame that we'll have to punish you for not listening to directions."

Madison went to respond, but before she got the chance, a sharp sting ran across her ass cheek. She turned around and caught Christian's wolfish grin.

"Still want rough?" he asked her.

Unable to deny the surge of wetness that had spilled from her with the spank, Madison nodded.

"I want more than that," she said. "Now, what's a girl got to do to get laid around here?"

Ryder chuckled. "She's got to open that mouth for something other than sassin'," he said.

Madison did as she was told, parting her lips to accept his cock. She tongued the head, enjoying the way it pulsed under her touch. Aching for more, she sucked him deeper and Ryder brought one hand to her hair, holding her head steady to pull with slow care from her mouth before sliding all the way in again. He kept up that rhythm and Madison was so consumed by the heat and desire flooding her at being taken from this angle by this man, that she nearly forgot about Christian — until he slapped her ass again. *Hard.*

"I can't wait to fill you up on both ends," Christian said. "I can't wait to feel your tight cunt squeezing me while Ryder fucks your throat."

Madison moaned around Ryder's cock, Christian's words turning her all kinds of hot with images of being filled and fucked by both of these gorgeous men.

"But first," Christian continued, "I want to see how red I can turn your ass, because you haven't been listening to us at all, sweet little cock slut, and bad girls get punished when they don't listen."

She didn't even have time to brace for the first slap, because it came while he was still talking, cutting sharp and intense across her ass. But the pleasure rolled through her in a great wave not a second later, and

Madison bowed, arching back toward Christian's cock to get more, something, anything to relieve the pressure building through her body. Hmm, she might just come from getting spanked while sucking cock. She'd never done that before.

"Oh, baby," Ryder groaned through clenched teeth. "Fuck, do that again, Christian—she's taking me so fucking deep right now."

Madison amended her earlier thought. She was going to come just from getting spanked and talked about like she wasn't even there, as she sucked cock.

But Christian slapped her ass again, all her thoughts fled and she could do nothing but ride the wave of pleasure and pain and everything in between.

"Didn't you once say that you wanted your pussy slapped?" Christian asked. "Maybe we should try that. But not right now. Right now I want to feel your cunt squeezing around me."

And with that, he slid his hard cock deep inside her spread legs until his balls rested at her ass. It stretched her, making her more full and more content than she had ever felt before. Then he slapped her ass one more time and the sensation of the pain with the fullness of his cock buried deep inside her sent an orgasm crashing over Madison so hard that she lost her footing, her eyes squeezing tight, her body rocking and riding and thrusting until she was reducing to trembling, whimpering murmurs, desperate and unclear.

"So fucking hot," Christian growled. "I love the feeling of you coming around me, around my cock. Will you do it again? Will you come for us while we fuck you in two holes at the same time?"

Without a fucking doubt.

Christian and Ryder set a maddeningly slow pace, unwavering, even when Madison rocked back and forth into them, as fast and hard as she could. But they just continued to tease until at last they both loosened, succumbing to their desires, a little faster, a little harder, a little rougher. They fucked her hard and she took and gave in equal measure until the rise of her pleasure mounted higher and she climbed right along with it, desperate to take both of them along this time, to give them just a little of what they had give to her, and she pressed and pushed and rode until she was bucking for all she was worth and Ryder was full-on fucking her face, just like Christian was fucking her cunt.

He brought his fingers around to her swollen clit and the smallest touch still had her writhing, needing, wild and losing control by the second.

Then he slapped her pussy.

It happened in slow and fast motion at the same time. The floor fell out from under her and Ryder's cock surged one more time before he unloaded deep in her mouth, as Christian thrust, thrust, *thrust,* before emptying himself into her. Madison rode, pleasure racing through her, before it was reduced to slow mini-tremors vibrating along her entire body.

"Are you okay?" Christian asked. They both helped her to stand to her full height and she nodded, her mind still a little fuzzy and thoughts still far away.

"More than okay," she whispered, enjoying the pleased expressions on both of their faces as they watched her. Christian withdrew from her body, grabbed a few tissues from his pocket and cleaned her off. Madison readjusted her skirt then brushed her hair out of her eyes. Ryder grimaced.

"You might want to tie your hair up," he said on a small laugh. "I think it's pretty obvious what we've been doing in here, if that look is anything to go by. If Micah or Dec takes one look at you, they'll know exactly what took place in the barn behind the stables."

"Good call." Madison combed her fingers through the tangled strands of hair before she was able to knot it into a loose braid. She checked her skirt one more time, fixed her top and looked up at both of the men standing beside her. How had she ever thought either of them intimidating? Now, she felt nothing but comfort and joy and happiness in their presence — *definitely still dangerous, then.*

"Listen, I wanted to go talk to the woman at the bakery stall for a bit," she said, because she *had* wanted to speak to the woman at the bakery stall and because she felt the sudden clawing need to get away from Christian and Ryder before she spilled her guts and said something that would bring this whole delicious little fantasy to an end. "I'll catch up with you guys in a little bit, though, okay?"

Ryder looked just a little skeptical, like he wanted to know *why* the bakery stall and why she hadn't invited them to come along, but Christian played her savior and just nodded.

"Just don't go running off with any other cowboys," he said, smiling one of those rare, real smiles that changed his whole face. Her favorite smile.

"Not a chance."

Before she could help herself, she brushed a kiss across first Ryder's cheek, then Christian's before slipping out of the barn door and back into the bustling fair without another backward glance.

Chapter Twelve

Christian had gotten halfway across the barn and toward the rest of the fair when Ryder's voice snapped through the air like a whip.

"What the hell was that about?"

When Christian turned around, Ryder had his arms crossed, the intimidating scowl on his face one that had long been reserved for his father and misbehaving livestock. Not that Christian hadn't ever fought with Ryder before. They'd scuffled and tumbled more times than he could count, sometimes drunk, sometimes pissed, sometimes both. They'd given each other plenty of black eyes over the years and more than one broken nose. But the expression on Ryder's face now, and the strength of his stance, told Christian that the coming altercation had nothing to do with a game of cards, a waitress or unmanaged teenage boy angst. Whatever Ryder was pissed about right now seemed to go a lot deeper than that.

"What the hell was what about?" Christian asked, confused as all hell. They'd just spent the last thirty minutes having mind-blowing sex with an incredible woman — what the hell could be wrong?

Don't pretend you don't know what's up his ass. It's the same damn thing up yours.

So what if it is? The whole thing was temporary and label-less and they never, ever needed to have this conversation, nor the fight that was simmering on the horizon just a few feet away from him.

"'Don't go running off with any other cowboys'?" Ryder's expression was tight. "What does that mean?"

Christian clenched his fist at his side, ready to start swinging if it came to it. Ryder maybe had more muscle, but Christian was the faster of the two in hand-to-hand, so it would be a pretty even match.

"So what?" Anger filled Christian for the first time. "So what if I don't want her to go running off with other men? Shouldn't you be happy about the suggestion? I've seen the way you look at her and I know you don't want to let her go —" He had plenty more to say, but Ryder interrupted him with a shove, sending him two feet out of the barn door and into the dusty alley between the fair and the farm it was on.

"I don't look at her any way," Ryder growled. Oh, Christian knew that growl. It had gotten him into as many fights as Ryder in college, when he'd had to go in and save his best friend's ass at a bar or party.

"You can lie to yourself, but you can't lie to me." Christian shoved Ryder back a step. Ryder took the step forward again and they stood face-to-face, chests nearly touching. "You want that woman in your life and you *hate* the idea that she doesn't seem to want to stick around. You like her."

"Back off, Christian," Ryder said, his voice dangerously low. "I'm telling you right now to back off."

"I'm not going anywhere," Christian replied. "Clearly something is up your ass where Maddy is concerned and I want to know what the hell it is. You may be my best friend, Ryder, but I'm sure as shit not letting you hurt that woman."

Ryder sucker-punched him in the gut. It was rude and fast and it knocked the breath clear from his stomach. Christian gasped and Ryder shook his head.

"I'm not the one who hurts women," he said. "The bad boy is all your territory. Break their hearts and leave them behind — you do that. Not me."

Sure, he *had* done that. Twice, to be specific. It wasn't as though there was a string of women around the block just asking for his attention.

"What the fuck, Ryder?" Christian got his breath back and swung for Ryder's jaw. He missed as Ryder moved out of the way, but Christian got a decent blow above his shoulder and collarbone. Ryder staggered back a little, kicking up a plume of dust from the road.

"Don't 'what the fuck' me, Christian. You think I'm the one who looks at her that way? You should catch a glimpse of that dewy-eyed expression you make at her. Let's be serious here. No matter what, you care around her, you like her and think she's important. How I feel has nothing to do with that."

"Jesus Christ, Ryder — it has *everything* to do with that. Don't you fucking get it? She won't have just one of us. It doesn't work that way. It's all or nothing. Use your fucking head, *doctor*." He pushed Ryder in the shoulder, the injured shoulder, one more time and this time Ryder landed a punch to his jaw instead of his gut and Christian fell back a step.

Then it was all-out battle, feet kicking up a storm of dust and rocks in the long aisle of people, arms and legs flying out at odd and concerning angles. Christian got in a crack to Ryder's jaw and Ryder landed one more punch to Christian's gut before they were both rolling around in the dirt and dust, scratching and fighting like they hadn't done since they'd been seventeen years old.

Then, just after Christian had got Ryder into a deep headlock and Ryder then pinned Christian to the ground, two pairs of shoes appears in their line of vision.

"Up, both of you. Now." Deckard McCormick might have been a happy-go-lucky guy most of the time, willing to flirt with anything on two legs, but when he used *that* tone of voice, there was no question in anyone's mind how he led a successful search and rescue team, saving lives and protecting people all the time. Two strong hands gripped Ryder's shoulders and pulled him off Christian, and two more dragged Christian up off the ground. When they were both standing at last, Christian turned around to see that Micah was holding him at a safe distance from where Dec was holding Ryder.

"What the fuck, guys?" Micah asked, in the low tone that somehow had a way of making a guy feel bad for what he'd just been caught doing. "It's about her, isn't it? Jesus Christ…" He sighed then nudged Christian forward. "Talk. Now."

Dec did the same with the Ryder until he and Christian were standing perhaps a foot apart.

Christian rolled his head back on his shoulders and let out a low, earth-shaking sigh.

"I like her, man." His voice couldn't be said to rise above a whisper. "I like her for a lot more than just the sex and just the temporary and all that. I've never liked a woman this way before and I know you like her, too."

Ryder sucked on his teeth and when he spat, blood flew out. Christian grimaced. It was obvious he'd never meant for it to go down like that. Ryder was his brother, his best fucking friend in the whole world, the guy he'd die for without question. But Maddy Hollis had a hold on him that he just couldn't shake and the truth was, he knew deep inside she'd never stay for just one of them — if she made the choice to stay at all.

"Yeah, man," Ryder said, his voice tart. "I like her too. A lot."

"Shake hands, both of you," Dec said, that same authoritative tone to his normally easy voice. "Now."

Ryder stuck his hand out first and after a long moment Christian reached out and accepted it. He sighed. "I just... I dunno, man. I was hoping for once we might be able to do something on our own. Does that make sense? It's always been us through everything, but I never thought this part would be us, too."

As if at a distance, Christian registered Dec and Micah stepping back, allowing them to have this conversation without an audience. Ryder pulled him into an embrace, tough and rough, just like the man himself, but telling, too.

"So what?" Ryder said after a minute. "We've done everything else in life together and we've succeeded, survived, whatever it took to get to the other side. There's something about Maddy, Christian. I couldn't tell you what it is, but I feel more for her than I've ever felt for anyone, and I have to be honest, it scares the shit out of me."

"It scares me, too," Christian admitted, his tone low and quiet. "It's been less than a week and she has us both wrapped around her finger." He glanced back to see if Dec and Micah were getting off on their whole true-confession thing, but the other two guys, having believed that Christian and Ryder were done with their little WWE scene for the day, had hightailed it, giving them space.

"We have to tell her everything," he said. "All of it. She needs to know the truth about Mason leaving us a stake in ownership and the loan and everything. And she needs to know how we feel about her, too. I want to ask her to stay."

Ryder nodded. "Let's ask her to stay. Together, after we've told her everything else. I don't want her to find out we've been keeping the agreement with Mason a secret."

Christian wiped his sweaty, no doubt bloody hair out of his eyes and felt a little lighter in the chest. The sooner they got this all over with and cleared away, the sooner they could tell Maddy how they felt and ask her to give them a chance to prove themselves good enough for her.

"Yeah. I don't want her thinking we seduced her to stay long enough for us to sign the papers with the bank." He was about to say how that would never have been their style in the first place and that they should both feel a little shitty about it—he sure did—but his stomach dropped like a fucking anvil and no words escaped.

Maddy stood just at the end of the lane, barely visible through a small clearing of trees, and it was so much more than clear that she had heard them.

"I guess that's it, then." Maddy's voice flatlined, the sound of it like a punch to the gut. Sure, they should have been honest from the start, but it hadn't taken half a minute for them to both him and Ryder to realize just how colossal a mistake they had made. Hell, they had just agreed to come clean about everything. No way she would believe that now, though.

And why the hell should she, when she'd been so honest, so open about everything, especially about her dickhead ex-fiancé, who hadn't treated her the way anyone deserved to be treated, but most definitely not Maddy. Judging by the expression on her face, she'd take her ex over them right now, and the truth of that was a knife slicing his shattering heart.

"Maddy..." He took a step forward, but she backed out of the clearing and into the lane. The hurt in her eyes turned to something far more dangerous, a firewall of anger neither he nor Ryder would be able to breach.

"Oh, no." She shook her head, her tone hot with rage. "You don't get to call me that. No way do you get to call me that." She stepped back, toward the larger fair, toward the crowds and the safety that wasn't them. He hated that she no longer felt safe with them, even as he understood exactly why.

"While we're on the subject of hard truths, I was going to tell you both that I'm considering turning Holmwood into a wedding venue for extra income and leaving the California event scene behind. See, that's what I was talking to Mrs. Potter about, how I might carve out a career for myself here, a *life*." She paused, looking at them like Christian looked at shit on the bottom of his boots.

"More fool me for thinking either of you might want to be involved in that life. Guess I don't need to worry about that, since you two seem more than happy to fuck me over any way you can. Isn't that right?" The smile she shot him was full of venom and it hurt worse than any snakebite.

"We were going to tell you," Ryder tried. Out of the corner of his eye, Christian saw what he knew to be panic on Ryder's face, the same panic Christian felt bursting in his own chest. They had barely known this woman a week, but she was becoming something important to them that transcended that shortness, something they both agreed was very much worth holding onto.

"After you got the loan from the bank?" she asked, her voice bitter. "After you bought the ranch out from under me, while you were *literally* under me?" Her scoff was self-admonishing to the core. "Well, go ahead. Buy your part-ownership in the ranch. I don't give a damn." She shook her head, steam practically spilling from her ears, her face red and eyes swelling with hurt.

"After everything I told you about Joshua and my parents…" She divided her fury between them. "You both know what I've gone through this week. Jesus *Christ*, you told me you'd take care of me. You told me to *trust* you, that you'd stop whenever one of us felt uncomfortable. Well, here I am, saying *stop*." She turned and stalked down the lane.

"Madison, where the hell are you going?" Ryder called.

"I'm getting a ride home," she said. "I don't really want to be around you guys right now."

Then she was down the alley and into the throng of people, leaving Christian feeling like he'd just swallowed a cement truck. He looked at Ryder, who had gone a little pale in the face of her admission, his expression saying everything Christian felt. They needed to fix this and they needed to do it fast, because once she left, there'd be no way in hell they could get her back. It was all of a sudden the most important thing in the world that she didn't leave.

Chapter Thirteen

Madison was proud of herself. She made it all the way to the bedroom, shut and locked the door, kicked the blasted boots across the floor and sat down on the bed before bursting into tears. She wasn't a crier, not as a rule. She hadn't even cried when she'd found Joshua. But overhearing Christian and Ryder, men she had felt some inexplicable connection to over the past week, discussing in an offhand manner how best to keep her *distracted* while they bought the ranch out from under her made Madison feel sick to her stomach. She hadn't expected declarations of love—that would have been insane—but something was growing between them, something a little more than sex, more than friendship.

Or so she had thought.

It turned out she was just absolute shit at picking men.

For a moment, Madison considered calling Lily, but if she were being completely honest, she *so* didn't feel like explaining to anyone else how much of a fool she was.

No, she needed to keep busy, keep her mind off the ache blooming behind her heart and the overwhelming sense of shame and hurt.

A small sound from under the bed started her and a second later Lucy jumped up, landing in a pile of fluffy gray limbs. She looked up, her eyes devoid of that cat condescension, and climbed into Madison's lap, snuggling her head against the inside of Madison's knee. It seemed everyone—herself included—wanted her to stay here, except the people she most wanted to miss her when she was gone.

No more wallowing. No more self-pity party. Time to take action. First, she grabbed her phone and made plans to go home. Good, there was an eight a.m. flight, which meant she could be ass-out of Triple Diamond before the sun was all the way up—far, far away from Christian Harlow and Ryder Dean before they could do any more damage.

Damn good thing I didn't quit my job yet. Sure, she'd get ranch profits soon enough, but for now she needed stability and structure—and her job was nothing if not time-consuming. Downtime was just a way for her to beat on herself a little longer for the stupid decisions she seemed to keep making.

A distraction would be great right now. She'd gotten her work done during the day, finished her book on the flight over, and didn't have wireless in the house, since she hadn't bothered asking about the password. *Negative points for another dumb move.* Madison was considering springing for an unlimited data plan when she caught sight of a brown box sitting on the bedside table.

Mason's photos—the pictures of Mom.

She grabbed the box, careful not to jostle the kitten, and settled crossed-legged on the bed. When she lifted the cover off the box, there it was, right on top, a faded photo of her mother as a child. If Madison got up from the bed, she'd be able to see the same tree out of the window, though, of course, it was much bigger now. Ellena Hollis — at the time Ellena Westerly King — had been a beautiful child. Unlike Madison, she was fair-haired and blue-eyed, just this side of too thin, and smiling.

Madison placed the photo down with a gentle hand and reached for the next. It showed a slightly older kid with his hand wrapped around her mother's shoulder, their twin expressions of joy and mischief so similar that Madison couldn't doubt that this was her uncle Mason, the man who had owned the Triple Diamond, the stranger who had left her everything.

The siblings, and Madison's young, unfamiliar grandparents, aged through the photos. High school graduation and prom photographs, images from the summertime, with the sandy-haired kids growing into young adults, moments frozen in time — canoes on the lake, smiling faces in the big farm fields of vegetables, state fairs and Halloweens and Christmases.

Madison's eyes burned as she turned over each picture with care to read the date, imagining her mother and her stranger uncle — not such a stranger anymore — growing up on Triple Diamond. *What a life that must have been.* Madison had known her mother grew up on a farm. She'd heard the stories throughout her life, of the animals and the open fields, and rising before the sun was full up, but Ellena hadn't specified the details and certainly hadn't mentioned that her ranch was one of the biggest in the state of Montana, or that it was worth several million a year.

At the bottom of the box was an old journal. It was leather-bound and clearly well-loved, and Madison almost felt bad about prying, but her curiosity to know more about the few family members she had on her mother's side was overwhelming, so she cracked it open, her touch careful and tender.

A gentleman's agreement, the first entry began, dated three decades prior in neat cursive.

Father has promised me the option of buying a substantial piece of ownership in the ranch. He says if I buy it, rather than inherit it, I will have a better understanding of its value. The price is fair. If I ever have sons, this is how they'll get their shares of the ranch.

Just like Christian and Ryder. He'd given them the chance to buy a section of the ranch so they could feel like it was in fact theirs. Had Mason felt like they were his sons? Why hadn't he ever married? Ever contacted her after Ellena had died?

She continued reading, following the chronology of his first years of ownership. He didn't write often, but each passage was full of love for the ranch. Then, her mother's name jumped from the page, almost startling her.

Ellena swears she'll run away with him. Father doesn't approve, but she doesn't care. He says if I support her, he won't allow me to buy the rest of the land. I don't give a damn about that, except I want a place to offer Katherine McCoy when I propose – a home, a good job. If Father takes the rest of the ranch from me, what do I have to give her besides a mean old man playing landlord?

So, he *had* loved a woman. Madison flipped to the next entry, dated a week later.

I found out why Ellena refuses to stay. She's pregnant. She's going to start showing soon. She told me never to tell Mother and Father, but if she doesn't leave with Eckerd soon, they'll figure it out. I tried to tell her I was sorry, but I don't think she understood. If Father ever finds out about any of this…
Note – I asked Katherine to marry me.

Typical man, didn't write whether or not she said yes. Still, the dates were growing nearer to her own birth and an ache grew in Madison's heart at the new knowledge that her mother had fled home and her family in order to bring her into the world. It was sad and hopeful all at the same time and she grasped for every detail of her mother's short life.

The journal passed through several months without any entries, followed by a few years of notes about the ranch. A date from right around her sixth birthday jumped out.

Katherine is pregnant. We've been trying so hard and it's finally happened. I wish we could share the news, but everyone is gone now. I wish I knew where Ellena was. She hasn't called or written since I told her I wouldn't fight Father. Seven years I've missed her, but now Father's gone and it's just Katherine and me.

A lump lodged in Madison's chest, part sadness for the broken family, *her* broken family, and part fear, trepidation for what was to come. And, six months later, it did in wrenching starkness.

Just me now. She fought so hard, my wife. She fought for both of them.

Aching with the heartbreak of it, Madison continued reading through the dutiful notes of ranch events and jobs, until another post grabbed her attention, several long years after the last.

Ellena is gone. There was a crash. Eckert's brother will adopt the child. Ellena named her Madison after me, just like she said she was going to. I thought my heart couldn't break any more. I really did.

She didn't cry. Perhaps it was the simplicity of his words, or the knowledge that another person mourned their passing as she did, the solidarity making her strong, but Madison didn't cry at those simple little lines. And the idea of being named for this heroic uncle she'd never met gave her strength, so she just nodded and continued reading.

Caught a couple of rascals trying to steal my truck at the store. Offered them a job instead of calling the sheriff. They seem like good kids and I know the old man Harlow. I know the old man Dean, too, but that's a strike against, not for. He's as mean as a dog, that one, and if I can be the reason a kid gets out of that house, I will.

Despite all the hurt and sadness, Madison's chest glowed warm. She wished she had known her uncle, wished she could have asked about her mother, about their childhoods, about everything. Wished Ellena and

Eckert Hollis were still here, still able to hold her close and tell her everything was going to be okay.

The boys are good workers. They've been here for nearly four years and I've offered them money to go to college, if they continue their jobs here on the ranch for five years after they graduate. They've both agreed. After that, I want to offer them a gentleman's agreement. I haven't forgiven my father for so much, but he was right about buying the land. It's so much more valuable to a person that way.

I'm writing the will this afternoon. I know it's early yet, but I've seen how quickly and quietly death can come from the shadows. I've been in touch with Eckert's brother. What isn't going sectioned off for Ryder and Christian will go to Ellena's daughter, Madison. She deserves a place full of memories, good ones. I want to see her, to know her, but I don't think I can. Not yet. Maybe one day.

I'm proud of Christian and Ryder. Not to put too fine a point on it, but they're good men, the both of them. Rough around the edges, sure, but hardworking, good men. I hope they decide to buy their sections of the ranch. They deserve it.

There were a few more pages, but Madison couldn't read any more, not with the contents of her heart crumbling into a thousand pieces, not with her uncle's memories flooding her mind. *How* could she sell Triple Diamond, when it was the only remaining tie to her mother's childhood and the uncle she had never met, but for whom she was named, the one who had left her almost everything? But then, how could she make Christian and Ryder leave? They belonged to this ranch as much as Holmwood Manor and the lake behind the barn. They'd tilled the land and sweated in the summer sunshine.

The knowledge that her uncle had cared for them as if they were his own sons made Madison's heart ease just a little. She was still leaving first thing in the morning, still working out the kinks of ranch ownership from a million miles away, where there was no chance of her running into either of the distracting and ultimately hurtful men.

But it seemed, from the pages of history, that people tended to sacrifice an awful lot where Triple Diamond was concerned. If they had in truth believed she planned to sell it, well, Madison could *almost* understand their actions. She just wished it hadn't been at the expense of her still fragile confidence and recently broken heart.

She placed the box aside and climbed under the covers. Lucy crawled in beside her, snuggling with her butt high in the air until she had made a nest for herself in Madison's embrace. That small, innocent kindness almost made her lose it. As a rule, she excelled at keeping order and control. Normally, her life was a series of boxes and straight lines. But with the end of her engagement, the inheritance and everything that had happened in the last few days between her and the men who ran Triple Diamond, Madison's mind was a mush of madness and confusion.

Frustrated, she fell back into the pillows and heaved a sigh. She was exhausted, mentally and physically, and had to be up early to get to the airport in time for her flight, but there was no way she'd fall asleep like this. Instead, every time she closed her eyes, Madison saw the image of her mother as a young girl, playing under the maple tree.

Chapter Fourteen

The sun didn't even pretend. Instead of an early orange glow, the sky remained a petulant dark blue and stars still hung high above her head when Madison looked out of the window early the next morning — or late the same night, in fact. She'd barely slept a minute the whole night, memories of her family turning into memories of the time she had spent with Ryder and Christian. Her dreams became the recollections of waking in Christian's arms, of the conversation she had shared with Ryder in the barn, the scent of aged wood and fresh hay weaving into her mind. So many scents she could grow used to so easily. She dreamed of their camping trip and the day at the fair and the mornings they had shared breakfast together. It hurt to remember the recent past as much as the distant.

Waking alone, or rather, rousing alone, since she hadn't ever fallen fully asleep, sucked and it made Madison grateful for the late hour and the dark sky. If the weather was as bright and beautiful as it had been the day before, with shards of golden sunlight stretching across the bed, she would have felt even shittier than she did right now.

Because I don't want to leave this place.

The truth had plagued her all night. She wanted to stay the summer—or longer—at Triple Diamond. Wanted to find every crevice and corner where she could sneak through time and into a memory of her mother. She wanted to find more photo albums. Wanted to look through what had once been Ellena's bedroom, see the clothes she had worn when she was young, the toys she had played with, the books she had read.

And she wanted to start a business here—her own business, away from the corporate world and the demands of the city. She wanted to follow the dream that had sent her into event planning in the first place all those years ago, here—turning Triple Diamond into a location for weddings and events.

But it wasn't just the memories of her mother lingering in the shadowed corners of the old ranch or her desire to start a business that had her questioning the decision to run. It was those stupid men, too. Though she hated the truth and each fresh shard of pain that came with it, Madison couldn't deny that whatever had sparked between her and Christian and Ryder felt...unfinished, somehow. She wanted to rage against them, but the words in Mason's journal and the growing connection she felt with the ranch went a long way to easing her fury where their deception was concerned.

She sure as shit didn't *forgive* them. They were nowhere near that. But a tiny part of her *almost* understood.

And since we're admitting hard truths, I'm going to miss them. Which was fucked up, but also true. Everything else — and there was a *lot* else — aside, people didn't engage in three-way love affairs, not in the long-term. But somehow it had all felt so normal, so *simple*, as if cooking dinner together and sharing beers and conversation and sex wasn't all that different with three partners rather than two.

Not that they were her partners. Because they weren't. Hell, they weren't even her friends.

She slung the bag over her shoulder, still heavy with documents she'd not even more than glanced at. Those could wait. First, she needed to get out of Montana, needed to clear her head about this whole thing. After a few days, it would be a lot easier to make the important decisions.

Madison glanced at her watch. *Shit, no time for self-pitying dilly-dallying.* She sped up on the stairs and exited through the side door toward the not-so-white-anymore BMW.

Juggling all her bags, Madison stepped out into the fresh mountain air and closed the door behind her. But when she turned around, she stopped dead in her tracks, heart frozen, breath caught. They were standing in the driveway right before her. Ryder leaned against a classic blue Ford pickup truck and Christian had one hand on the leather seat of a chrome and black Harley. Madison shook her head, hoping to knock some sense around in her brain. Maybe she had fallen asleep after all. That seemed a lot more likely than this actually happening.

"I have a flight to catch," she stated, shouldering her bag higher, like a shield. "Please move your vehicles."

Christian crossed his arms. He was formidable when he did that, all strength and just-leashed power. Though Ryder intimidated her a little with his mystery and depth, Christian was large, tattooed and standing next to an also large Harley.

And I still think he's sexy, after everything. Nice survival skills, Maddy. Madison. Damn it.

Maybe, in a different time and a different life, she would have ridden him on the back of that bike and for more nights than just one.

"Maddy," he said, his voice gentle. "Stay."

Her blood ran hot and she dropped her bag to the ground, reveling in the crunching sound it made on impact.

"Now why the fuck would I do that?" Rage burned through her and she clenched her jaw and her fists. "So you can use me again? So you can screw me in every way possible? So you can get another chance to hurt me?"

"You know we never meant to hurt you," Ryder said in a quiet tone. Hurt shone in those pretty boy blue eyes. *Ha.* They didn't get to be the hurt ones here.

"I *don't* know that," she said and most of the frustration in her voice was directed inward. "I don't know anything about you guys. My naïve brain thought we had some kind of connection, but obviously I was being stupid. *Again.* Now, if you'll excuse me, I have a flight to catch."

Neither of them moved. "We tried to tell you last night," Christian said, "both of us feel that connection, too, Maddy. There's something here between us, somehow, some way. Don't tell us you're willing to just walk away from whatever it might be."

Her chest grew tight, each breath a little labored against the red-hot burn of panic and anger.

Maybe they're telling the truth. Maybe they want me to stay.

Ha. Fool me once…

"Why should I trust you?" she demanded, pushing down the kindling hope in her chest. Angry tears caught at the back of her throat. "Why the *hell* should I trust you? The second I turn my back, you'll buy the whole damn ranch out from under me."

"No," Ryder said. "We won't." He took a tentative step forward. When he looked down at her hands, Madison thought he might take them in his own, but then he hesitated, as if not certain if he was allowed to touch her. *Fine.* He wasn't allowed. "The truck and the bike, they were our collateral for the bank." He dug into his pocket and pulled out a pink slip. The car's title. "If giving you this for safe keeping means you'll stay then I'll transfer the damn thing into your name."

Christian pushed off the bike and came to stand in front of her too. He pulled a pink slip from his pocket and held it out.

"Take them." He waved the bike title. "We're not going to buy this place, not if it means hurting you again. We don't want you to stay because we've tricked you into it. We want you to stay because we both like you. We want to help you start your business. Hell, we both *care* about you and we want to see where the future takes us. Together."

He looked up at her, his expression more intense and serious than she had ever seen it.

"I love you, Madison Hollis. I don't know how or when, but I damn well fell in love with you."

Ryder came up to stand beside Christian and swallowed hard. "I love you, too, Madison. We both do. We got into a pretty nasty fight about it yesterday, but we're here now, both of us together, and we're asking you to stay."

She let out a shaky sigh. "You're serious." It wasn't quite a question, but it wasn't sure enough to be a statement either. Because everything had gone topsy-turvy and Madison struggled to think rationally, to see past her desire to keep Christian and Ryder in her life, despite all the hurt they had caused in so little time. But Mason's journal resonated in her mind, a reminder that they were good men, that they'd almost been raised by her own flesh and blood. Of course, none of that was as important as the fact that they were standing in front of her and offering up proof they wouldn't try and go behind her back again, promising they'd never use her or lie to her, asking for a chance.

And she wanted to take that chance, wanted to because she believed them. She believed the wild, slightly panicked hope in their eyes. She felt sure that the rough men holding out their rough hands with those pink slips, proof of the commitment to their cause, wouldn't pull them back in a moment's time. She *knew* that they wanted her to stay.

"I..." The words were difficult to find amid the confusion of emotion. "I want to stay, too. I want to start the business. I want to know more about this place and my family history." She gestured around the ranch. "And I want to get to know both of you, to see where this all takes us. I want the chance to be your Maddy...because I think I love you both, too. I do. Christian Harlow and Ryder Dean, I love you."

And in that moment, she wasn't Madison Hollis, director of event planning for Daniels and Hark. She wasn't the orphaned daughter of Ellena and Eckerd Hollis. She wasn't anyone but herself, bare and suddenly fit to burst with joy. And in the presence of Ryder Dean and Christian Harlow, *herself* felt a damn lot like Maddy.

"Our Maddy," Christian said. He took her hands and pressed rough kisses to the back of her knuckles. "I could get damn used to the sound of that."

Ryder kissed the column of her neck and his soft, seductive touch made her mind go blank and heat surge down her whole body. She felt like laughing. This was one hundred percent insane. She was staying at Triple Diamond. She wasn't going back to San Francisco. She was giving this total madness between Christian and Ryder and herself a chance. *Oh boy, that's a hell of a lot to take in at once.*

"You're thinking too hard," Christian murmured against her ear. "We'll just have to try harder to distract you. Come on inside."

She followed them back into the house, needing to keep a hand on each of them, a touch to prove this was real—and it was, down to the delicious scents of breakfast that hit her when they got inside. Maddy pursed her lips.

"Very optimistic," she said. A huge stack of pancakes sat right in the middle of the kitchen table, with eggs, bacon and fruit around it.

"We were hoping you'd stay." Ryder's laugh and voice rang with honesty. "And if you didn't, we were planning to drown our sorrows in syrup."

Maddy laughed and plucked a strawberry off the plate. She bit into the soft flesh and it sparked against her tongue, indulgent and sweet.

"Syrup is sticky," she said. When she opened her eyes, the two men watched her with hooded gazes, lust evident in both their expressions.

"And delicious," Ryder said. "But I'd much prefer to lick it off your skin than a pancake."

He grabbed the syrup bottle and drizzled a thin line of confection across his finger. "Taste," he murmured and pressed his creation to her mouth. Maddy's blood pulsed with heat and need and she parted her lips and sucked his finger deep, almost failing to register the syrup over the taste of Ryder and the surging pleasure she got from sucking him, any part of him.

"Jesus," Ryder groaned. "You're so fucking sexy when you make that noise."

Maddy realized belatedly that she'd been moaning around his finger. With one more long suck, she pulled free and looked each of them in the eye, meeting their intense gazes. Then she took Christian's hand, tangling their fingers together as she bent her head up to kiss Ryder. The embrace was long and hot and lingering, stirring that desperate fire within that she now knew she couldn't resist. She wanted this man, both of these men, with a lust that overtook her, made her ache and burn and need more than anything in her life ever had.

Ryder broke the kiss and Maddy had almost no chance to look at Christian before he brought his mouth down on hers. He plunged his tongue deep and hot into her mouth and Maddy clenched her pussy, longing to feel him plunging deep and hot far more intimately. Then Christian picked her up and placed her on the counter, still kissing her. Ryder popped open the buttons on her dress shirt and ran heated caresses down her exposed skin.

She spread her legs, desperate to take more...of *something*, and Ryder got her shirt open and pulled her breast free from her bra before he started sucking on her swollen nipple. Maddy moaned into Christian's mouth and arched to meet Ryder's touch, just as something cool and not a little sticky touched her breast.

She broke her kiss, her laugh husky "Did you just pour syrup on my breast?" she asked, knowing the answer by the smug, lusty expression in Ryder's eyes. When she looked up to Christian for support, he just smirked, dangerous, promising.

"I'm one hundred percent on the Maddy-covered-in-syrup train," he said. "Lie back, city girl. Let us devour you."

Well, how the hell can I refuse an invitation like that? Instead, she pulled her shirt all the way free then did as she was told. Oh, it was hot as hell to be on display like this, two desperate gazes trained on her body. Then they weren't just looking, but touching, too. Ryder ran a thin line of syrup from her swollen breasts down her stomach, stopping just at the top of her pants. Christian wrapped one of her legs over his shoulder and started undoing the button on her dress pants. Ryder sucked and nibbled at her collarbone, running sticky sweet kisses across her swollen nipples. Fuck *yes*.

Ryder disappeared for a moment, and when he returned to her line of sight, he plucked a ripe, red strawberry from the bowl in his hand.

"I could get off just watching you eat strawberries," he said. "Have a bite."

She moaned, the soft flesh of the fruit bursting into sweet taste against her tongue. Juice spilled across her lips and Ryder lapped at it, toying with her mouth, making her murmur nothing words against his tongue.

"What, baby?" he asked. "What do you need?" As if the sexy bastard didn't know. Maddy arched into Ryder's touch and Christian's fingers, which were now toying with the waistband of her panties.

"Someone please *touch* me," she groaned, already feeling pleasure and pressure building up her body, making her pliable and desperate for more. "I need… I need…"

Christian swiped one finger down the line of silk and she growled. "More…" Her voice was a husky sob and when he ran his finger over the wet material again, she didn't hold back her scream.

Then Christian slid her pants off her legs, leaving her black pumps on her feet, before he bent down to his knees and pressed a heated kiss to her covered pussy. He slipped his tongue across where she needed him most and her mind blanked, pressure building higher and higher without release.

Ryder pinched her nipple between two fingers and the sharp bite of pain made her arch into Christian's touch, bucking and needing.

"Are you going to come in his mouth, sugar?" Ryder asked. "Gonna scream while you spill your juices all over his tongue?"

The words turned her already burning need explosive and Maddy nodded. Somehow.

"Tell him what you want…" Ryder's voice was controlled and demanding, even as he slid a ripe strawberry around the curve of her breast in a slow, erotic caress. He plumped the flesh of her breast with the fruit before pressing it across her nipple. Then, his intense gaze never leaving hers, he slipped it between his lips and sank his teeth into the fresh berry.

Maddy's eyelids fluttered at the erotic sight at the same moment as Christian brushed her swollen clit with his tongue. Her orgasm caught her off-guard, sent her careening into pleasure and she screamed and grasped at the countertop, spotlights of need and desire bursting before her eyes.

She came down from her high, her body still shaking with the tremors of her release. Christian stood up between her legs and the expression in his dark eyes filled her body with heat all over again, a volcano building up to a new explosion.

"You're so fucking sexy when you're coming in my mouth," he said and she believed him. "Tell us what you want, Maddy. You're in charge."

For a moment, words failed her, but then she took control and asked for what she wanted, what she needed. "I wanna be filled up," she said. "Filled up and fucked hard." She reached across the counter and unbuttoned Ryder's pants then pulled down his zipper.

Down the counter, Christian unzipped his own pants in deliberate, slow motions. A moment later, Maddy freed Ryder's cock from his pants, not surprised to find him commando under his jeans. She gave his thick, hot erection a languid stroke and he surged under her touch. Maddy licked her lips, aroused by the hot-as-sin image of his large cock in her small hand.

"Ask nicely," Ryder said, his waning control evident. "And I might just give it to you."

In that moment, Maddy admitted to herself that she quite liked being told what to do. "I want to suck your cock," she breathed. "Please?"

He didn't hesitate a moment before sliding his thick, leaking head across her lips. Maddy leaned out to lick the pre-cum around the crown of his hardness and Ryder hissed.

"Go slow, Maddy. I'm real close," he murmured. "Licking syrup off your breasts fucking does it for me."

She didn't respond, just sucked his cock down until he bumped the back of her throat, a heavy, salty weight against her tongue. Ryder let out a string of curses — or prayers — and steadied himself against the counter. But before she could tease him further, Christian spread her legs wide, placing her feet on the counter. Then he slid one finger deep inside her.

"Oh, you like sucking cock, don't you, pretty girl?" he murmured. "It gets you off. You're so fucking wet." He stroked inside her one more time before pulling back. Then, to her surprise, he moved his finger just that little touch lower until it hedged the entrance to her ass.

"Is this okay?" Christian asked, his voice serious. "Tell me to stop." But Maddy didn't want him to stop. She wanted the press of his fingers against her tight, aching hole, the need to feel something everywhere overwhelming her, and she pressed into his finger, already so wet with her pussy juices. His digit was large and it was a tight fit, but the feeling of his finger inside her ass was fucking erotic as hell and a fresh wave of heat spilled from her pussy.

"Christian, she's fucking losing it." Ryder's words came out on a harsh groan. "Oh, *fuck*, baby…"

Christian didn't wait. He sheathed his cock with one hand and lined up at her entrance, finger still deep in her ass.

Then, before she could arch up and meet him, Christian slid his full hardness deep into her pussy, until he was buried balls-deep inside her and she was stretched and full and oh-so overwhelmed.

Christian started moving and Maddy sucked Ryder's cock deep, following the same rhythm and bringing her hips up to meet Christian's cock and fingers. Her whole body burned, needing more pressure, even as she knew it would push her right over the edge. Her nipples throbbed and her belly glowed with lust and each time Ryder pulsed deep and erratic into her mouth, her ache buzzed and pleasure built on the eroticism of his cock dragging against her tongue. Christian pulsed deep inside her, nearing his own release, and they were getting closer to the edge, the precipice of their insane desires.

Ryder broke first. He pulled his cock free of her mouth and spurted long jets of cum across her bare chest, growling a deep, carnal sound. He dragged the leaking head of his cock against one swollen breast, just as Christian's cock hit her *right there* and Maddy lost herself. The floor spun out from under her and she screamed, taking Christian's cock, once, twice, once more, before he flooded the condom deep inside her, riding her hard and fast, her pussy clenching around him, their orgasms overtaking them.

Maddy fell back against the countertop, panting and spent, her whole body buzzing with the aftereffects of her pleasures. She sighed and looked up to face the two men — *her* two men.

"You've convinced me to stay," she murmured, her voice husky from screaming her release. "Now, how does this all work?" A pulse of satisfaction glowed deep within her at the sight of just how spent Ryder and Christian were.

"First, it starts with a shower." Ryder picked her up off the counter. "Then it starts with breakfast. After that, it starts with a tour around your ranch, making love to you, business meetings, more making love to you, dinner then…" Maddy looked over Ryder's shoulder at Christian and he smiled.

"It's a little untraditional." Christian shrugged. "But it feels real, doesn't it?"

Maddy pressed against Ryder's muscled chest, inhaling the scent of him and the scent of her body on him. Yes, he was all-too real. Christian's tangled sex hair was all-too real. The very intense pleasure still racking her body was all-too real. This was all real — including the very real feeling of deeply loving these men and the Triple Diamond Ranch, despite the short amount of time she had known either. Maddy had the feeling that the more she got to know the land and the men who tilled it, the realer and deeper everything between them would become. She couldn't wait.

Epilogue

Maddy paced, walking through the large tent at the far field as though one last glance at the rows of softly decorated chairs or the expansive view of the lake leading into the mountains could possibly change anything. Which, of course, it couldn't. A dark sky rolled in from the west, looming like an ominous horror movie shadow in the near distance. The tent poles shivered in the breeze and Madison resisted the urge to find half a dozen railroad spikes and nail them into the ground with double the force herself.

"Calm down."

She whipped her head around so fast she was surprised to find it still attached. Christian stood at the far end of the aisle, looking just a little amused at her state and clearly making an effort not to show it. She appreciated the try, somewhere deep in her frazzled brain.

"It's my first wedding, Christian." She looked down each row of chairs, not even sure for what. "I need this to go as smoothly as possible and I have two bobcats on the loose, a storm rolling in and a mother-in-law who claims to be allergic to *old barns*." The electricity buzzed in her brain and she ran down her mental list again. The caterer's arrival, the makeup and hair arrival, the guests' arrival — those not staying at the newly converted Holmwood B&B, that was.

She made her way down the aisle to him and he scooped her into his arms, preventing any more quick head movements or frenetic pacing.

"Look at me."

She did, if with a little reluctance. There was too much on her mind, too much to do right now to take this moment and enjoy the feel of his warm body wrapping hard around her, giving her safety and comfort and peace of mind. Maddy squinted and pulled back.

"You look nice," she said, directing the comment first to him then to Ryder, who was just coming up the curve of the hillside and into sight. "You both dress up well." For the average suit in San Francisco, their outfits might have been considered dressing down, but both Ryder and Christian looked like different men in their form-fitting slacks, Ryder's pants in a deep charcoal and Christian still dressed in black, and nice their button-down shirts, straining against the muscles underneath. They almost looked respectable, even without jackets and ties, like the wedding guests were sure to wear. But Christian's hair was pulled into a tight queue at the back of his neck and his tattoos were tucked away. Ryder's windswept hair had been tamed and he was for once wearing a shirt, which pretty much put him halfway to respectable.

"You like?" Ryder asked, wrapping one arm around her waist and leaning down to kiss the top of her head. *Oh, hell* yeah, she liked.

"I'd like those outfits even more on my floor," she said with a grin, loving seeing them like this, her wild men looking cleaned up and polished, and only she would know just what was underneath.

"That'll have to wait, sugar." Ryder wore a knowing grin. "I came up here to grab you because the mother of the groom is insisting that we change the direction the chairs are facing so the sun won't be in her eyes. I told her there was a storm *and* a tent, but I think she'd probably listen better hearing it from you." He raised his brows. "She threatened to call a cab and go back to the airport, so you might want to hop to."

Maddy nodded, smiled at both of her men then turned for the house — or rather, what had used to be a house. Her plans to turn Triple Diamond into a wedding venue had gone better than expected and had included converting the massive and stunning Holmwood Manor into a working B&B. Among the list of caterers, flower shops and justices of the peace, she had outlines in place for setting up horseback riding and wine tasting weekends that would fill the rooms when there wasn't also an event going on. It had only taken six weeks to properly turn Holmwood into a bed and breakfast, and it appeared — with the exception of the bobcats, storm and mother-in-law — like the trial run for the wedding venue was going surprisingly well.

She found the groom's mother in a chair by the fireplace and was able to comfort her in a matter of moments, though, there would be little comfort for the bride in a lifelong relationship with that woman. The caterers came and set up and Maddy felt a little like a traffic conductor during rush hour. She sent the makeup and hair team to the bride's room on the third floor, then directed the troublesome groomsmen to the pool table they had arranged in the bar.

"You did a wonderful job, Maddy," Bethany Orsen said, when Maddy knocked on her door a few minutes later to inform her that the guests were taking their seats. "This place, the food, the rooms — everything is just the way I imagined it to be." She hugged Maddy, then settled in for her final makeup touches.

Everything she imagined. What do you imagine for a wedding, Maddy?

Not like she hadn't thought about it. Hell, she'd been *engaged*, though not for long enough to make an official start on the wedding plans. But she hadn't thought much about it, not about the colors or the gift bags or the aesthetics or her dress or any of the things that women imagined when thinking about their wedding day.

Could she even have a wedding day? She didn't doubt for a second that her relationship with Christian and Ryder was one for the long haul, more so now since they were now business partners, roommates and lovers — and succeeding beyond all expectations at all three. In her mind, the idea of a life without either man was impossible to comprehend, heart-breaking, even in the hypothetical. But how could they possibly get married? How could she legally marry one man and not the other? The question nagged at her, running circles around her mind as she showed the guests into the tent and directed the caterers with plates and champagne glasses.

Bethany was beautiful walking down the aisle. She radiated joy and nervous excitement and Maddy stood at the back of the tent, watching over the affair with a mixture of happiness for the woman and a little forlornness that she might never get the chance to take that walk herself. No, her relationship wasn't what could be called traditional, but the love she shared with both men felt true and real and old as the land they now stood upon.

And Wolf Creek didn't seem to mind. They didn't hang their unorthodox relationship on a banner for all to see, but those who mattered knew and the hands and larger-by-the-day staff who worked the now ranch and wedding venue had either walked in on a delicate scene or would at some point. Sure, they got the looks, but one of the nice things about Wolf Creek was that folks were real good about minding business that was theirs and no one else's.

Bethany came up to stand before her fiancé, Will, and the ceremony began. It was short and beautiful and the rain held off just long enough to get the guests into the barn for dinner and dancing before cracking open the sky with lightning and torrential deluges. Not that she had any intention of saying so to Bethany, but the rain was a good thing — the crops had been looking a little dry.

The party was a big success, perfect for her first time at planning the type of events she really wanted to be doing. The world in San Francisco had been challenging and interesting, but this was where her heart really lay.

And here, with these two men, now coming up behind her.

It was late. The rain had at last stopped, but Maddy didn't turn away from the scene stretching in a thousand miles before her. Hours earlier, the guests had all turned in for bed and the rising fog of mountains and rivers against the dark blue sky was intimate and safe. All this land made her feel so much safer than her little apartment in San Francisco ever had.

The air was brisk and she believed Christian to have been right when he'd said autumn was coming early. She shivered, just a little, and two strong arms wrapped around her back, providing so much warmth and comfort that Maddy would never feel cold again.

"You did it, boss," Ryder said. "Kick ass trial run, I'd say." His voice held a smile and it was contagious. Even though she felt a little maudlin, for whatever reason, Maddy couldn't deny that their first go — her first go — at the new business was a resounding success.

"You guys made it possible." She turned to each of them and kissed their rough cheeks. Ryder had shaved that morning, the soft bristle already filling in. Christian hadn't. He'd been growing his facial hair a little long and she liked it. *A lot.*

"You made it all possible, Maddy," Christian said. "You make so much possible."

She nuzzled into his neck, enjoying the warmth she found there.

"We do it together." She meant it to the tips of herself, her toes, her fingers — every last piece filled with joy and gratitude for bringing her to them.

"What's the matter, sugar?" Ryder said. "You don't sound like you just had an overwhelming success."

Maddy nodded, not even a little surprised that he had picked up on the slight sadness in her voice. It was the same magic he used with the barn animals, an innate sense of knowing when something was off. She pulled away from Christian and, beautiful dress be damned, plunked down into the grass, staring out over the edge of the hillside.

Christian and Ryder followed suit. Ryder tilted his head against her shoulder and Christian leaned his back up against her, both waiting for an explanation.

"Does it ever bother you?" she blurted into the dark air.

"Does what ever both us?" Ryder traced small, calming patterns against the bare skin of her shoulder and arm.

Maddy gestured in frustration. "That we can't have...this." She indicated the tent and the tables. "We'll never be able to have this." She hated the frustration in her voice, hated that it even mattered. She had these two amazing men in her life. They worked together. They lived together. She didn't need some sort of special title to believe it was all real — it was, and it was incredible for it.

"Baby, who says we can't have this?" Ryder asked. Both men came around to face her, their eyes and smiles aglow in the moonlight, power and emotion exuding from them.

"How could we?" she asked. "Last I checked, bigamy is still illegal in the United States."

Christian choked out a laugh. "Fuck that. We've been making up the rules ourselves for a damn long time, Madison. We're not about to start following someone else's."

She perked up at the sound of her full name, something Christian hardly ever called her. But before curiosity could take over, both men climbed to one knee and looked at her, love and adoration in their eyes.

"Maddy, we love you," Ryder said. "No, it's not traditional and it's not going to be as easy, either, but it's important enough to us that we don't care about those things."

Christian nodded. "We want to make you ours, really and completely. The ceremony won't be legally binding, but we thought we could maybe convince you to do a hand fasting." He pulled a small box out of his pocket and opened it and her heart stopped beating, her chest too filled with joy to do anything other than burst. Which she did, right into tears.

"We planned to do this tonight," Ryder said, "and you gave us a good segue. Say, yes, Madison Hollis. Say you'll be our city girl for life."

Christian slid the ring out of the box and onto her outstretched finger. The Triple Diamond logo, a band with three diamonds, the one in the middle just a little bigger than the other two, and stretching around the ring were slightly raised, engraved mountain ridges. Triple diamond, three gems in a row.

"Of course, I say, yes!" she said. "I love you, Christian. I love you, Ryder. I want to have a life together, a future."

"I love you, Maddy," Ryder said.

"I love you," Christian echoed.

Then she kissed both of them stupid, fit to burst with the joy of it all. Tomorrow, she'd call Lily. Tomorrow, she'd pick a date to settle into the planner. Tomorrow, she'd do a thousand things, once the madness had passed. But for right now, all she wanted to do was take the hands of the two men who loved her most in the world, and she wanted to pull them up the hill and through the kitchen of their house and up the stairs and into their bedroom, where she wanted to make love to them all night. So, Madison Hollis, Maddy, Sugar, City Girl, owner of the Triple Diamond Ranch and the Holmwood Wedding Co. did just that.

Want to see more from this author?
Here's a taster for you to enjoy!

Triple Diamond: Wild Flowers
Gemma Snow

Excerpt

"We've got a scent!"

Axel was trying hard not to get too far ahead of Micah to see, and Micah did his best to keep pace, following the large and very determined golden retriever down a steep incline, clenching his thighs and lowering his center of gravity to avoid sliding on the wet, fallen leaves that coated the Clark Mountain Range of Glacier National Park, at the edge of the Montana–Canada border. Axel, on his four legs, was doing a much better job holding his grip on the ground, but Micah had no desire to go sliding off the edge of the mountain and into the depths of the canyons below, so he whistled a command and the dog slowed enough for Micah to catch up.

Still, they kept an admirable pace and quickly came to a plateau of flat ground. High above, at the top of the ridge, Micah heard his partner Dec — Deckard McCormick — approaching with Rosie, Axel's sister. Rosie kicked up a pile of leaves on the approach, clearly picking up on the same scent Axel had.

"Anything down there?" Dec shouted, the sound catching and echoing off the many flat walls of the mountain range.

"I think I saw a cave," Micah called back, straining to look around the corner of a large boulder that jutted forth from the ground and mountainside. "Give me a second. I'll let you know whether or not to come down."

Dec gave the affirmative then Micah crouched low to peer around the edge of the boulder.

Oh, shit.

That wasn't just a boulder. That was the edge of the fucking mountain, looking down over a sheer two hundred foot drop to the canyon below. For a fleeting, horrible second, vertigo caught his senses and nearly dragged him to his knees, making the sky and the high trees waver and tilt.

But Micah put a steadying hand on the rock wall and took a deep breath, settling the sky firmly above him and the ground firmly below. He commanded Axel to stay put—not that he needed to. Axel was a damn smart dog and knew better than to go canyon jumping. Then Micah lay flat on his stomach, damn near hanging over the edge of the mountain, to look around the boulder's protruding side.

There was definitely a cave on the other side, a yawning, darkened mouth, gaping right over the valley. The question was—was there anyone in it?

"Hello," he called, his breath labored and caught, what with his stomach pressed against the ground. And he was still pressed against the ground. He had to keep reminding himself of that. The stones and wet leaves that rasped against his forearms, giving a slight fall chill in the mountains, were all real. For this moment, at least, he wasn't plummeting toward certain death below.

"Is there anyone in the cave?" *A pause.* The silence was weighty, colored by the sounds of raptors flying overhead and wind rippling through the trees that towered high above the ground, giving Micah a very odd sense of perspective as to exactly how far up in the sky he was.

Oh, about ten thousand feet…

But now was just about the worst time to calculate the distance it would take to kill a grown man, so he focused his attention on the solid ground and his mission and called out again. "This is Lewis and Clark County Search and Rescue Agent Micah Ellison, I repeat, is there anyone in the cave?"

A sound. It was barely even a real sound and if he hadn't been trained by the very best to determine the difference between human and nature, he might not have heard it. But there it was, a whimper catching on the wind, the softest, shuddering inhalation of a very terrified child.

Chloe Robinson. Female. African American. Six years old and approximately thirty-nine inches tall. Last seen Tuesday, October Eight. Amber alert issued Wednesday, October Nine.

She'd been gone a week. In the world of search and rescue, a week was no better than a month was no better than a year. It was true what they said about forty-eight hours. Truer still when the Montana mountain ranges, of which there were many, were known for being unforgiving and merciless. Micah knew all about that first-hand.

But there was no denying the signs of life coming from the other side of the boulder. After nearly a decade of doing this job, Micah knew the sound of a frightened child all too well and unless the universe played some pretty hairy tricks, the girl on the other side of that sheer drop down to the valley was Chloe Robinson.

"Chloe," he called out, hoping the sound would carry and not get lost on the wind, as any calls he made toward Dec and the team undoubtedly would. "Chloe Robinson."

The sound of her fearful whimpering increased and when he called her name again, this time she answered him. *Thank fuck for small victories.*

"How do you know my name?"

But that was the way of kids, wasn't it? Find them hidden in a darkened cave in the middle of a mountain range and they want to know how you know their name.

"Your mom and dad told me," Micah replied. "See, they've been missing you and they sent me and my partner Dec out to see if we could find you with our dogs, Axel and Rosie. Do you like dogs, Chloe?"

A small sniff echoed across the gap, then, "I have a dog…at home. Her name is Daisy."

Micah sighed in relief. Good, she was talking, which meant she wasn't too dehydrated to function or too badly injured. He hoped.

"Well, Chloe, I'd really like to get you back home to Daisy, okay?" he said. "Now, I'm going to talk to my partner, but I'll be right back…"

"No!" she shouted the word before he even finished his sentence. "Stay. Don't leave. I don't want to be alone anymore."

Micah nodded and as carefully as he could, reached for the radio on his utility belt.

"Okay, I'm not leaving," he said. "But I'm going to talk to him over the radio, okay? I just want to let him know that I found you, all right?"

She sniffled but agreed and Micah brought the radio to his mouth, doing his damnedest to think about Chloe, the brave as all hell six-year-old in the cave, and not the freaking mountainous drop right below his face.

"Dec," he radioed over. "She's here." The radio crackled in and out, then cut out completely, plunging the mountain's edge into silence that suddenly felt a whole hell of a lot colder and lonelier than it had a minute ago.

Or maybe that was just the clouds rolling in overhead. *For fuck's sake.*

Okay, okay. He'd dealt with hairier situations than this and he was damn well going to get that girl out of the cave if it was his last act on earth and all that. He sent up a prayer to as many of his gods as he could remember in the moment then called back to the little girl.

"Just you and me now, Chloe, okay?" he said. "Now, I'm going to hook my belaying chord to a tree on this side of the gap then I'm coming over to you. You can talk to me. I can hear you."

He stood and stepped a foot in from the edge of the cliff, allowing himself one deep breath before walking over to the thick oak tree growing sideways out of the mountain. He tested a branch with his weight, finding it thick and sturdy, before tossing the end of the rope around it and securing the knot that he had been tying since he was about Chloe's age. He tugged on the end attached to his security belt and, satisfied, returned to the edge of the mountain.

"How did you end up here, Chloe?" *Don't look down, Micah.*

"I got lost," Chloe said, only a slight sniffle to her voice. *Christ, this six-year-old little girl has bigger balls than I do.* "I hid in the cave and fell asleep then there was a huge lightning storm. I woke up when all the rocks crashed."

On closer inspection, Micah could tell that a big section of the mountain had broken free, creating the gap between him and the cave where Chloe was hidden. She'd walked into the cave and hadn't been able to walk out, unless she was some sort of New Age Jesus.

"Well, you're very brave, Chloe," he said, testing the rope one more time. "I'm coming over now, okay?" And before she could answer him, he began the slow, one-foot-in-front-of-the-other walk across the large yawning mouth of the valley. He didn't dare lift his feet, but rather scraped them along the mountain's edge, making rock and dust crumble, and he gritted his teeth to keep from following their path with his eyes.

He'd been working for Lewis and Clark County Search and Rescue Team for nearly six years and he never got over that feeling of being suspended over the incredibly far valley below. Even two decades later, memories still plagued him, very nearly paralyzing a man who was otherwise incredibly good at his job.

But before Micah could give in to any of those fears or panics, his feet touched down on the other side, grounding him against the dirt and mossy leaves, and there he was, at the entrance to the cave.

"Chloe," he called, his voice soft and gentle. "It's me, Micah. Do you want to come out of there now?"

She emerged, her movements slow and wary. Her clothes were dirty and her hair had all manner of sticks and leaves tangled in the curls, but she appeared otherwise unharmed, and Micah let out a low breath of relief. "You did a good job hiding here, honey," he said. "Now, I'd like to bring you home to your mom and dad, okay?"

She nodded and sniffled. "Okay." It seemed that the bravery that had gotten her so far was just about tapped out. Well, fine, she was allowed to be a kid again. It was no longer her responsibility to get home safely.

"Okay," he repeated. "Now, I'm going to hook you into this harness, then we're going to slowly walk across that gap. My dog, Axel, he's on the other side, waiting to meet you."

She nodded and, before either of them got the chance to freak the fuck out about trekking across that massive drop again, Micah had her hooked into the front section of the harness built for rescue missions just like this one, and he was scooting them alongside the mountain's sheer face, shuffling his feet and trying to keep breathing.

Then, mercifully, they were back on solid freaking ground, both inhaling more breath than necessary. Micah slowly, carefully, stood and picked Chloe up, hoisting her onto his hip. He unhooked the harness from the tree and whistled for Axel to follow before beginning the trek back up the hill to where their point camp was located.

It only took a few minutes. Axel kept a good pace and Chloe weighed about as much as a couch cushion, and before he knew it, the blue tent from their rescue rendezvous camp loomed into sight. A brief, weighty silence stretched across the mountain. Then all hell broke loose.

Her mother screamed then both of Chloe's parents were sprinting toward them, Police Chief Cade Easton and two of his deputies hot on their heels. Mr. Robinson took Chloe from Micah's arms and both of her parents were hugging her and touching her and making sure she was still in one piece. Micah tried to fade back, but Chloe grabbed the arm of his windbreaker.

"Thank you, Mr. Micah," she whispered, her bright eyes shining. Her parents both looked up at him with the same glowing adoration.

"Thank you, Micah," Mrs. Robinson said, as Mr. Robinson stuck out his hand and shook it hard, before bringing Micah in for a bear hug. Then they were gone, carrying Chloe over to the medic tent, and Micah stepped back to watch them walk off into the distance. He should have been relieved. They hadn't expected such a happy ending for Chloe and they'd been lucky, more than lucky.

But still, the ache in his chest didn't dissipate and he knew it was no longer fear that made him feel so heavy and forlorn. Axel whimpered at his side, and Micah dug into one of his pockets to give the dog a treat. He loved Axel and Rosie and the other search dogs they kept at the Black Reef Survival Camp, but dogs were a poor substitute for family, for parents, for children, for *people* who loved a person unconditionally. Well, dogs were what he was going to get, a truth he'd come to terms with a long time ago. Family wasn't in the cards for him, not the kind of family Chloe Robinson had. No, Axel and Rosie, they were what he got, so he'd damn well better be happy about it.

"Hey there, Superman," Dec said, coming up behind him, Rosie hot on his heels. "Or should I say Spider-Man? That was some gravity-defying shit you did down there."

And Dec McCormick. Of course. He counted as Micah's business partner, search partner, family and best friend, all rolled into one not-giving-a-damn package of good-old-boy humor and charm. Dec was one of the few people in the world who knew just how much Micah hated heights, but, as with most things, he played to the lighter side of the situation.

"I can't be out-balled by a six-year-old," Micah said, suddenly feeling very weary. He followed Dec away from the camp and toward their cabin a little way down the mountain. If Cade needed them to give statements, he knew where to find them.

"Ain't that the truth," Dec said. "Come on, let's get a beer."

Micah nodded, but glanced back up at the Robinson family one more time. Growing older with a houseful of dogs and their business and Dec McCormick by his side definitely wasn't the worst life a guy could have.

Home of Erotic Romance

Sign up for our newsletter and find out about all our romance book releases, eBook sales and promotions, sneak peeks and FREE romance books!

About the Author

Gemma Snow loves high heat, high adventures and high expectations for her heroes! Her stories are set in the past and present, from the glittering streets of Paris to cowboy-rich Triple Diamond Ranch in Wolf Creek, Montana.

In her free time, she loves to travel, and spent several months living in a fourteenth-century castle in the Netherlands. When not exploring the world, she likes dreaming up stories, eating spicy food, driving fast cars and talking to strangers. She recently moved to Nashville with a cute redheaded cat and a cute redheaded boy.

Gemma loves to hear from readers. You can find her contact information, website details and author profile page at https://www.totallybound.com

www.ingramcontent.com/pod-product-compliance
Lightning Source LLC
Chambersburg PA
CBHW020419180626
46812CB00003B/1061